PENGUIN BOOKS

LOVE CURRY

Pankaj Dubey is a storyteller who keeps meandering between various forms of media. A bestselling bilingual novelist, he is also a screenwriter and film-maker. He has written all his books—*What A Loser!*, *Ishqiyapa—To Hell with Love* and the latest *Love Curry*—in Hindi as well.

A recipient of the Best First Published Book of an Author Award at Lit-O-Fest, Mumbai, Pankaj Dubey has also won the Youth Icon Award for Social Entrepreneurship for initiating India's first street film festival for children in slums and villages—the Sadak Chhaap Film Festival—in Karnataka in 2010. He later won the Creative Leadership Award at Lit-O-Fest, Mumbai, for his campaign to increase readership by taking his novels to twenty small towns and cities in India.

Pankaj Dubey is known to address sociopolitical issues with quirky humour in his writings. A law graduate from Campus Law Centre, University of Delhi, he also has a master's in applied communications from Coventry University, West Midlands, England. He has been a journalist with the BBC World Service in London. He was among the three novelists from Asia to be selected for the prestigious Writers' Residency in the Seoul Art Space, South Korea, in 2016.

You can follow him on Twitter and Instagram (@carryonpd). To know more about him, visit www.pankajdubey.com.

LOVE CURRY

PANKAJ DUBEY

PENGUIN BOOKS

An imprint of Penguin Random House

PENGUIN BOOKS

USA | Canada | UK | Ireland | Australia
New Zealand | India | South Africa | China | Singapore

Penguin Books is part of the Penguin Random House group of companies
whose addresses can be found at global.penguinrandomhouse.com

Published by Penguin Random House India Pvt. Ltd
4th Floor, Capital Tower 1, MG Road,
Gurugram 122 002, Haryana, India

First published in Penguin Books by Penguin Random House India 2017

ISBN 9780143424505

Typeset in Bembo Std by Manipal Digital Systems, Manipal

Printed at Repro India Limited

www.penguin.co.in

1

She climbed on to him, casting off her silky, backless negligee. In baggy jeans, he lay waiting and watching her, smiling and increasingly restless. Skin met skin and it felt so warm and good. She kept slithering up and down him. No matter what she did or where, he simply loved it. So he gave her a free ticket to please herself. Kissing, cuddling, kicking and moaning, they spent the next half hour exactly the way they wanted. Then fell back on the bed, drained but replete.

It was quite a high bed with an extra mattress and fluffy pillows. Topping it was a quirky bed sheet that flaunted a Japanese girl on it, hand-painted. Mood lighting and seductive music added colour to their frolic. And they were not alone here. Printed feng shui dragons, hawkish paper birds and glitzy butterflies watched them make out from the walls on which they were pinned. Tribal masks, wind chimes and wooden aircraft swayed overhead, enjoying their foreplay. Posters of pretty women winked and teased from every corner. In this room like no other, they sure had company.

She scrunched a portion of the girl painted on the bed sheet and asked with a pout, 'What's she doing on your bed?'

Staring at the girl on the bed sheet, he told the one asking him, 'She's in queue!'

She hit him then. Playfully. He pulled her down hard and locked her tight in his arms. Her face, inches above his own, dazzled him. Looking deep into those eyes, he blew at her lightly, making her smile. And look even prettier, if that was possible. Minutes passed and they stayed that way, drowning in each other. Then his muscles began to ache. Beauty can bewitch, but weight can kill. So he turned sideways and eased off her luscious kilos on to the welcoming bed sheet.

Sprawled next to him, her eyes left his face to rove over his bare chest. Her manicured fingers traced the path her eyes had forged. Learning every nook and cranny of his well-carved torso, she paused at the imposing eagle tattooed over his heart. It was special, eye-catching—and more than just a tattoo. It was a statement of all that he was.

She decided to make the eagle her own, and so she began to colour it with the red lipstick that was her constant companion, filling the dark eyes of the predator a deep red. He twisted, uncomfortable with her artwork. But she kept at it.

'Don't. You're hurting it.'

Brushing off her hand, he grabbed fistfuls of her coal-black hair and drew her face to him again.

'Kiss me, baby,' he hissed. Their breath mingled and the heat that was generated threatened to overpower her. She tried to resist even as he feasted on her mouth.

Sensing her holding back only incited him to grip her harder. He pulled her to him with sudden force, and she fell on top of him—and they fell off the high bed. Landing on the floor with a loud thud, they rolled with laughter, pointing fingers at each other.

'You can't even hold me tight?'

'You can't even smooch me right?'

Fighting. Complaining. Laughing. They tumbled into each other. And resumed what they had been doing, forgetting their fall.

Till a loud knock interrupted them; a knock so insistent that they were forced to unlock their lips even as the door stayed locked.

'Yeah?' he let out irritably, after letting go of her.

'You a'right, man?' The loud concern floated in through the locked door. That was Ali, his housemate.

'Yup, not dead yet.'

Satisfied with this answer, Ali left. And so did their enthusiasm. There was nothing left for them to finish. The spark was gone, and so had their rhythm. Sweat was all that remained.

Picking up his T-shirt, she wiped her face and slowly got up. Hauling himself off the floor, he walked up to the drawer that held his wallet, opened it and drew out some notes—featuring the Queen and her tight smile—and offered them to the girl.

She shoved the pounds hurriedly into the pocket of her jeans and peeked into the mirror to straighten her messed-up hair.

He ambled up to her for a last kiss. 'Zeenat . . .' he breathed.

Plucking out her red lipstick, she ignored his plea and got busy painting her lips a ruby red.

He kept waiting. She was done.

'Next time, Shehzad,' was her parting shot, before she went knocking on the door. In the same house. Another room. Another guy.

The door was half-open. She knocked gently and out came Ali, beaming, wearing his crisp cream *pathani* suit.

'Please . . . please come in,' he beckoned.

'Not today, Ali.'

'I made you some firni . . . just the way you like it . . . less sugary.' His voice was polite and low. Even as he spoke, he darted back into his room and brought out a silver tray, with a bowl of firni. The sweet might draw her in, hoped Ali.

'No, *janaab*, don't want anything sweet.' Zeenat was firm. 'Just give me the cash and I'll go.'

'Keema samosas then . . .' proposed Ali, pointing to the fried parcels on his tray. 'Have one.'

His insistence won out. Zeenat picked up a keema samosa and took a bite. Having got his way, Ali quickly took out an envelope from his kurta pocket and handed it over to her. A benign smile lit up his elegant face. Almost six feet tall, with long, brown hair slicked back to stay out of the way and a face that looked more mature than its twenty-two years, Ali was a fine man by average standards, but distinctly lacking in the seductive quotient

Not sparing him another look, Zeenat pocketed the envelope and moved on to the next door.

She knocked, and getting no reply, turned the handle, only to find it locked. *Shit!* The fellow had replaced the internal locking door handle with another that locked on the outside. Shady bugger! Cursing her luck, she began to walk away, when a note stuck beside the door caught her eye. She pulled it out and read: '*Will have the money transferred by Monday. Yet to get my salary. Rishi.*'

That was Rishi Mathur. Like the character Mr India played by Anil Kapoor, in the Bollywood blockbuster of the same name, this Mr India had decided to go invisible too. Shaking her head, Zeenat decided it was time she too vanished from house number 104, George Street, Hill View, London.

She walked out, rich and free.

2

He came from Agra—the city of the Taj Mahal, a monument that stood for a timeless love. A monument that simply kept standing when his love had wandered off. No wonder he had left the city and its Mahal. Choosing England instead with all its apparent coldness. He wanted to be away from all that had always been with him. No one knew him here or cared to. But there was a comfort in this anonymity. It was only months after he shifted to house number 104, George Street, that some of his neighbours began to recognize him, or what little they saw of him. For he would leave in the morning and return only after it got dark. He could have been the nightwatchman for all they knew. No words he exchanged with anyone. No twitch of a smile to a face that looked familiar. His socializing was restricted to giving someone way if they were in a rush.

His name was Rishi Mathur, the guy whose door was locked. The occupant of the third room in house number 104.

A house that was almost a subcontinent, harbouring as it did three South Asian boys, flying the flags of India, Pakistan and Bangladesh. Besides the Indian—Rishi—docking in the house were Shehzad from Dhaka and Ali from Lahore.

Rishi in Agra had been quite a talkative fellow. This was a different version. No, the Queen wasn't to blame for this sudden, sullen silence. At the heart of the matter was a breakup. One he was finding difficult to chew. So he went quiet and fled to England. He had seen people go to London to study or to get rich. But he came to recover. People arrived here with big dreams. He landed with promises—three promises that he'd made to himself. Three promises that were perhaps the opposite of what any other immigrant from India would have made.

The first was to stay away from girls—especially the beautiful ones. He could not trust them now.

The second vow was to never return home. He would do all it took to make this island nation his new home. There was nothing waiting for him in India—and absolutely no one that mattered to his broken heart.

Thirdly, he would lie low. No soaring aspirations for him. No growth, no riches. He would not be the next British-Indian industrialist or Indian lord in Parliament. All he would be was a nobody.

It was easy to do the third thing. He simply didn't need to do much. The limelight ignored him automatically. High denomination pounds stayed away. The few notes he earned kept hopping in and out of his wallet. The heartbroken hero strived for no comeback as a happy success story. All he wanted and got was a corner seat in life.

No one knew what Rishi did, not even his two housemates. Shehzad from Dhaka and Ali from Lahore lived in the same house with him, but in blissful ignorance. Each one had a story of his own that each wished to keep to himself. Though they shared a subcontinent and now a house, the three were reluctant to overlook the fact that they came from three different countries. This fourth country that they came to live in however threw them together in more ways than one. For starters, they got branded 'Bloody Pakis' the second they set foot here!

In their three-bedroom house, the room in the middle went to Rishi. Shehzad occupied the one to his left. The Bangladeshi was almost twenty-three, but still had a somewhat wild streak, which was announced by the sheer number of tattoos covering his five-foot-eight-inch frame. No, he didn't need them to enhance his looks—he had plenty of those already. His angular face and curly fringe were a photographer's dream. The decoupage tattoos advertised the person he was—a question mark. No one knew what he would say or do next, not even Shehzad. Only one thing was reasonably clear—rehab would figure somewhere in his future! For, the fellow smoked up relentlessly.

What made him so unpredictable was an even bigger mystery. No one knew the painful backstory. It featured a father who was an airline pilot in his home country. But that was before he lost one of his limbs in a ground accident. The tragedy, however, didn't end there. His mother eloped soon after, forsaking his father for another pilot who was a friend of the family. The six-year-old boy was left behind with a handicapped father, a pit of a future and so many wagging tongues.

It wasn't a joyous start by any standard. Boiling inside with anger and hurt and not having anyone to vent his frustration upon, the boy sat for hours at his desk, digging his compass into the wooden head of the table, making hole after hole. That rid him of some of the shit pent up in him, and so he etched and etched, driving his compass on to the desk. Daily. The act soon became his comfort pillow, and in time, he found that all his emotions and pain flowed out in his etchings. Moving from etchings on desks to body tattoos was a natural course. His evolution as a tattoo artist was thus quite organic.

The room to Rishi's right was Ali's. The Pakistani was an assistant chef at the Nawab Balti, a desi restaurant in the Brick Lane area of East London. His unhurried air and polite demeanour often had a calming effect on people. Not that he wasn't emotional, but he kept it all bottled up, mimicking the stillness of the Thames most of the time. There was however a method to his saneness. He had to be this way to get what he had come for. Yes, Ali too had a story.

Legendary *dhabawallahs* of Lahore, his family name, fame and dhaba had fallen on hard times. Prolonged family feuds had driven away all customers and the *rupiya*, leaving the nihari specialists with a tandoor gone cold. That's what had forced Ali to migrate to cold and distant England. He had come to turn his wheel of fortune. Make enough moolah to restart the family dhaba. Nihari Badshah, he would call it. Soon it would be the talk of the town. Sending all tongues dripping and stomachs growling.

Ali was not one to only dream. He was willing to sweat it out in his Brick Lane eatery kitchen for as long as it took, whipping up lamb chops and kebabs. As long as he was cooking, he was happy. Sprinkling the spices, grilling the chicken, watching the biryani cook, inhaling the mixed aromas of ten different things—this was life, and it filled him with deep pleasure. It was almost like making love! Nothing could upset him here. No, he wasn't that barking chef, losing his cool over every little ingredient or error. Ali stirred his creations with a smile, lost in the art of his preparation.

This was Rishi's nest, boasting of an eagle-like Shehzad and the swan of an Ali. Sometimes fighting, sometimes cooperating; and at times, looking past each other as if they were air; all three soon learnt to live with one another peacefully under one roof.

* * *

The doorbell rang. It was the first day of the month.

On the doorstep of house number 104, George Street, stood Zeenat Amaan. She'd come to collect the monthly rent. This beautiful woman came calling because Mohammad Mullah, the house owner, and her father, told her to. He believed his daughter was his luckiest charm. So all money dealings had to happen through her precious palms.

Mohammad Mullah was an institution in himself. His life was straight out of Bollywood, with enough masala and intrigue to snap anyone out of their slumber. His daughter was his crowning jewel—his pride and joy. She held not just his heart but many more that came beating her way, taking some, kicking some.

Her appearance at the house ignited tumultuous feelings inside both Shehzad and Ali. The first wanted to bed her. The second longed to marry her. But this was just the beginning, a trailer of things to come. Shehzad and Ali stood drooling. And Rishi? He sat unmoving like an avatar of Vishwamitra. Life had bulletproofed that overrated organ throbbing near his lungs, making him immune to any degree of beauty.

Rishi led his life loyal to his three promises. Never losing sight of his vows on what to steer clear of. Buried in his work and god knows what else, he acted deaf and dumb until it became absolutely necessary to intervene. His housemates were quite okay with this. They were not really interested in knowing him more than he cared to tell. The Ali-Shehzad-Zeenat drooling drama soon matured into a full-fledged chase scene. Everyone seemed to be after someone—everyone but Rishi. Zeenat kept coming and going. And coming again. Shehzad kept throwing her come-hither looks. Ali kept dancing in the background. All in all, it was developing into a masala Bollywood film!

And then, her visits got more frequent. One day, she was sharing tequila. Another day, she was cooking brunch. Goofing with Ali one day. Cosy with Shehzad the next day. Chatter and more chatter filled the place, sparks flew. Rishi could see, but chose not to.

Zeenat liked having both men dancing at her feet. One oozed sex. The other spelt grace. It was a heady mix, flooring her, but confusing too. She liked floating on Ali's compliments. And crashing on Shehzad's bed. The Pakistani warmed her heart. The Bangladeshi made her hot and sweaty. Both messed up her thermostat way too much. One thing though left her cold—and that was Rishi. The sour and sullen housemate was like furniture to her—existing, but not overtly mattering in the daily scheme of things. Rishi was okay with that, and both tried to outdo the other in this game of indifference.

Zeenat Amaan was thrilled by the new complications in her life. Ali or Shehzad? Shehzad or Ali? Life was looking up for her. The Dhaka Romeo made her insides jelly. His angular chin, bunched and rippling torso, his unkempt hair . . . she couldn't have enough of him. Together they erupted like a volcano that had an overload of lava. On the other hand, small talk with Ali was like a soothing massage, gentle and comforting.

She felt secure under his wings. With Shehzad, things were electric. She was drawn. Pulled to him, she held on to Ali too, making a perfect triangle. The third angle in a love triangle is notorious for messing things up. This house was no different. Too many suitors in one house led to collisions—fiery ones.

3

The rented house number 104 in George Street belonged to Mohammad Mullah. The landlord lived exactly ten houses ahead, on the same street. Hailing from Gujarat, Mohammad Mullah was rightly expected to have come from a flourishing business background. All his friends had fathers running factories or exporting textiles, dealing in stones, salt or gems. But Mullah's background featured the tabla instead, because that's what his father taught in the local school. The little boy thus grew up dreaming big and loud of making a resounding name in the music industry one day.

Mullah moved to Mumbai the minute he grew up. He wanted to be a music director. And who had ever heard of music directors sprouting from Ahmedabad! Tinseltown it had to be, and so he went. But months went by . . . then years. Album after album got released . . . movies too, but all without

Mullah. He featured nowhere except in his dreams. Yet, he kept waiting. Hoping.

And god became kind to him one day. A troupe was to perform in London at a huge New Year show for Asians—*Jumma Chumma*. No, he wasn't to be their music director. Mullah was summoned only to play the tabla, and that too because the original tabla player backed out at the last hour. His walkout became Mullah's gain. And so the aspiring music director picked up his tabla, thanked his father in heaven for passing on his skill and lost no time in claiming his lottery ticket. It was the 1990s, and the show was riding on the success of superstar Amitabh Bachchan's latest Bollywood blockbuster, *Hum*. Mullah vowed to make it his launch pad too.

The troupe arrived in London with Mohammad Mullah and his pair of tablas and performed at the famous Wembley Stadium. Many Gujarati families had settled in this area and the air was intoxicated with the chatter and merriment of this community. Fafdas and theplas ruled the conversations. Inspired by the smells and stories of his community's strides in London, Mohammad Mullah's mind went on a trip of its own. He did play his tablas, and the show was a big hit. But what happened after the show was a bigger hit for him. Mohammad Mullah disappeared.

The organizers reported him missing and filed a police complaint. But found not even the shadow of the replacement tabla player. So the entourage returned to India without Mohammad Mullah, and they carried his tablas back with them in his memory.

To hide in the white island, Mullah picked up the many tricks employed by the other illegal immigrants. Years of hide-and-seek followed. Mohammad Mullah finally managed to evade all the authorities and create his space in the country.

He married Fiza Khan, a British-Pakistani woman. After the nuptials, Mohammad Mullah became legit and could settle down in peace, and eventually flourish, running a series of businesses, some legal and some not-so legal. The product of their union was a beauty called Zeenat Amaan.

Zeenat Amaan looked like an expensive cocktail—dressed, frilled and rightly measured. She grew up seeing the rise of Katrina Kaif to fame and fortune, and was duly inspired. So she joined Bollywood dancing classes. And then, thinking far ahead, enrolled for martial arts too—to kick that unruly fan who might stalk her once she got famous. She definitely was on track. But why the hell was she stuck with the name Zeenat Amaan? Blame it on the Bollywood fixation of her tabla-playing father.

One day, getting home, she pirouetted before Mohammad Mullah, holding aloft some notes and kissing them filmy style. 'I got rich,' she sang. 'Two-fifty . . . I got 250!'

Mullah's face bore a smile and a question. He couldn't help but delight in her happiness. But he was equally concerned about the source of her windfall.

'Zeenat?'

She flashed the notes right under his nose and crooned, 'From your desi boys, I got! Your rent, I got!'

Mohammad Mullah cleared his throat. A sure sign of disapproval.

'That was to go into the savings account . . . right?' His well-organized mind could not stomach this frivolity.

'Right! But then you named me Zeenat Amaan!'

Mullah raised his eyebrows.

'Zeenat Amaan's got big expenses. The name calls for big bucks to blow.'

Mullah had no words.

'Why did you do that? Why name me after her?' Zeenat asked with a pout.

He was angry, yet he hugged her. Doting on her and her pouting beauty. Such fights were common between them and they always ended the same way—her way. He threw a question. She threw a tantrum. He put his hands up and took a walk. She walked out with more money in her pocket, looting his kitty for her fashion fetishes. She was Zeenat Amaan—destined for Bollywood. She had to be stylish, and style didn't come cheap. Mullah knew he'd sowed the seed himself by giving her the name, so he indulged her. Like she indulged every single whim she had.

Mohammad Mullah's wife, Fiza, belonged to the elite class. Her father was a British Muslim blessed with more than enough name, fame, entrepreneurial talent and money. It had been quite a task for Mohammad Mullah to impress Fiza's father. His tabla skills and unsung musical background did not excite his prospective bride's father. It was only after he managed to identify and demonstrate some of his innate entrepreneurial abilities that Mullah could score some points with him. The whole procedure took no less than four and a half months. Once married, Mohammad Mullah doubled his business prowess overnight, learning every survival trick to beat the cutthroat competition. But he'd always had the aptitude. With what flair he had gone underground! And with what charm he had converted his illegal immigration to legal! No, sir! There definitely was no dearth of talent within him.

Mohammad Mullah shied not at exploiting his genius fully—learning and adapting and growing with an uncanny speed. The world now knew him as a dignified businessman and a doting father. His legal half, Fiza Khan, was a striking but surprisingly reserved lady. She exuded the assured air and attitude of having been born and brought up in London. Husbands like Mohammad Mullah, despite all their success, were often called 'imported husbands' because they had not grown up in England. Even their kids tended to relate more to their mothers. Zeenat, however, was an exception. She and her dad loved each other to the moon and back.

And like her well-organized dad, in no time, she too put in place all the zigzag elements in her life. Zeenat's universe and code of conduct were now very well defined. With Shehzad, the tenant from Dhaka, her chemistry was steamy. She was not sure yet whether she loved him. With Ali, it was different. She enjoyed flirting with the genteel chef from Pakistan. He was her pet poodle. As for Rishi, he did not figure in her galaxy. She cared not a hoot whether he was in London or Agra. Her scheme of life included variety for sure, but not to the extent that Natasha's had. This girl was her best friend, and what made her really special was her colourful ambition to bed at least one guy from all the 196 countries in the world. Zeenat calculated that she did not have that kind of energy to go global.

4

The living room sofa threatened to collapse tonight. Bearing the weight of a tense subcontinent, that too during a crucial cricket match, was more than what the three-seater was designed to take. While the Bangladeshi kept wiggling at one end, the Indian and Pakistani were jumping rather than sitting on it. Ali and Rishi bounced in joy or sank in despair with every shot or miss. Shehzad sat shirtless while the other two flaunted their national colours. Green T-shirt fought with the blue T-shirt over every ball. Air-punching. Screaming. Cheering. Abusing. They were waging an international war from their sofa in this house in London. Clashing more fiercely than the cricketers on-field. The Ali vs Rishi match threatened to get tenser than the India–Pakistan final playing out in Eden Gardens.

Ali shrieked and beat his cushion when Afridi hit a six—for once, he forgot to be genteel and polished. Rishi exulted when the umpire declared the six to be a four. Volumes rose, drowning out the commentators on TV. Shehzad sniggered from his corner seat. It was a treat for him to watch his well-behaved housemates morph into goons at the flick of a TV remote. All credit went to the subcontinental clash of the year—the Air Asia Cup. Bangladesh had already crashed out of the tournament, so the Dhaka boy's blood pressure was stable. But this Tom-and-Jerry sequence unfolding in the house today—the Pakistani housemate chasing the Indian specimen round and round the sofa to stop him from dancing at the fall of every Pakistani wicket—it was far too entertaining for the Bangladeshi to miss out on. It was so funny, he almost dropped his beer.

Ali had gone mad and Rishi was completely to blame for this sudden reversal of personality. He kept pushing his buttons right from the time the captains went out to toss.

'Fixed it, Ali?'

The chef kept mum.

Pakistan won the toss.

'See! I told you the ISI would fix it.'

Ali simmered.

Pakistan was batting, and Rishi kept bowling his own bouncers, citing statistics, rubbing it in about Pakistan not winning a single ODI series the last two years. Ali looked like he would implode any minute.

The South Asian party stayed glued to the screen till the fifty overs were complete. The Pakistani team had notched up a giant score. Satisfied, Ali made his way to the kitchen to start his biryani. He was making his special tonight. Shehzad and Rishi followed to help him. They had learnt to chop the onions, garlic and chillies, and grind the cardamom, and soak and drain the rice exactly the way Ali wanted. Every time Ali whipped up one of his specials, the boys were in for a treat. Tonight, however, Rishi was too fidgety to be of much help. Shehzad did his share and went back to his beer.

The Indian openers walked out to bat and the housemates plopped back on the tortured sofa. Ali was in an exceptionally good mood. Too many runs on the board and his biryani simmering close by gave him a rush that made him sing.

'*Dil, dil Pakistan . . . dil, dil Pakistan . . .*' Ali kept chanting, swaying left to right, smiling…till he got on even Shehzad's nerves. Rishi was at boiling point. One rash shot after another was sending the Indians back to the pavilion faster than the TV expert could fully analyse. Like the rebound shot in a game of carrom, the Indian batsmen walked out to bat and on the follow through, walked right back in to the dressing room. The umpire looked like he was working harder than the men in blue that night.

Rishi clutched his head and stared blankly at the tragedy unfolding before him. Ali had gone hoarse singing, and substituting song for dance, he was now flailing his arms up and down and twisting to some silent tune. Shehzad was in a fix now. There were two shows beaming at the same time. What should he watch—India's tragedy on the screen, or Ali's comedy in the room?

The last over was being bowled. Rishi had gone mute and Ali was mumbling a prayer. Even Shehzad sat on edge, thrilled by this cliffhanger. India needed ten runs to win and Pakistan just a wicket. It could swing either way. Then Umar Gul took a catch and Kohli, as Ali put it, became *gul*. The match was over and India had lost.

All hell broke loose. Ali leapt up, did a frenzied dance and went on a hugging spree. First Shehzad. Then Rishi. Then Shehzad again. Rishi sat shell-shocked. To Pakistan of all countries! How could India? He needed time to let this sink in.

'Ali, I'm starving,' Shehzad announced, making his way to the kitchen. 'Watching you two jokers has stoked my appetite.'

'Anything and everything stokes your appetite,' replied Ali, following him. 'You were born hungry, bro.'

Rishi wanted no part in this conversation or bonhomie tonight. He got up to go to his room—and collided with the pot of hot biryani Ali was bringing in. Ouch! Twice that evening, the Indian had got scalded.

'Watch it, man,' Shehzad was by him in a trice. 'You lost a match, not the love of your life.' But Rishi was not ripe for friendly banter just then. He collected himself and made to take off, only to be grounded again by a beaming Ali.

'Biryani's here. Where're you off to?'

Rishi was fuming. *First they massacre you on the field, and then they want to shove a fragrant biryani into your face!*

'Janaab!' Ali stopped him with a hand.

The Indian lost it then. 'Don't want your goddamned khana or *tana*! Let me be.' And he shut himself in his room.

Ali looked at Shehzad. Shehzad looked at the closed door. This was not the Rishi they knew. Their quiet housemate was not known to throw a tantrum, especially when there was biryani at stake! Ali decided to barge in with a plateful. Victory making him more magnanimous. A Pakistani win was not easy for an Indian to swallow. Ali knew, he needed to be extra sweet.

But Rishi was still seething. And the sight of the Pakistani blew him up like a bomb. 'Out!' he screamed, driving away both Ali and his biryani.

Shehzad consoled the stunned Pakistani in his own fashion. 'Forget it, bro. He's got a brain fade.' This classic excuse bandied by an Aussie captain to explain his unsportsmanlike conduct had the boys tittering again. The party soon resumed without the sulking Rishi. The fight—both on-field and off-field—had upped their appetite, and the rice was almost gone in minutes.

Glancing at the closed door, the Pakistani declared with a wink, 'Let's cross the LoC and eat the Indian's share too!' Guffawing, the boys polished off the entire bowl.

5

Another night without food! The kitchen was full of mutton and dal, but that was of no use. No one ate or offered another a plate. Wanting to eat or not to eat, after all, is all in the mind. Of course, it's the stomach that digests the food. But first, you need to have the heart and mind to eat! And theirs was consumed with debt.

Haji Sahib's dream was about to end. It was a rude wake-up call for the entire clan. Bickering uncles and aunts had ruined what Ali's great-grandfather had built with pots of love, sweat and skill eighty years ago. It was Haji Sahib who imported the nihari tradition from Chandni Chowk to Lahore. It went on to rule the hearts and tongues of all in Lahore. '*Laanath ain in ulloo ke pathon par!*' Ali cursed. This third generation was bent on cutting down the tree that gave them fruit and shade. *Fucking idiots!*

Ali fumed and broke into a sweat. On a cold, wintry night in Brick Lane, Ali was bathed in perspiration. How could he salvage the situation? The dhaba had been their lifeline for generations. Hotel, they called it, Haji's Hotel, serving the best nihari this side of the border. Every visitor to Lahore got to hear of it even before they set foot in the city. And these idiots were ruining it. Loan after loan they'd taken to open branch after branch of their family dhaba, mindlessly diluting the quality, reputation and income. Thinking big, but without brains, they were driven only by greed and jealousy. Ali's uncles had butchered the family's pride and biggest asset.

Now, Ali had to deal with not just these illogical uncles but the ever-present banks too. Only after Ali repaid them could he press the restart button of his life. And Ali had found a way—one that would lead to England, yet keep him close to his pots and pans. He would go and cook nihari in England till he earned enough to reopen his nihari hotel back in Lahore. Nihari Badshah, he would call it, he thought for the hundredth time.

The phone rang, intruding into his thoughts. Ali wiped his clammy hands on his apron and answered the call. There was no point dwelling on the past when the present beckoned.

'Ali?' It was Zeenat's mother.

Ali snapped to attention, forgetting that his prospective mother-in-law could only hear and not see him.

'Yes, Mumani?'

'Can you bring two kg of balti chicken with you? Got some guests tonight.'

The request warmed his heart. Thanking Allah for this opportunity to visit Zeenat's house, Ali quite forgot to respond to Fiza.

'Ali?' she said, checking to confirm if he was still there and could deliver. Satisfied, she hung up.

* * *

It was near closing time. Ali packed the parcel with care and was on his way, with dreams in his eyes and balti chicken in his hand. Zeenat was so aromatic and heady. Like his chane ki dal. He couldn't have enough of either. Increasingly, Ali found he liked hanging out with her. With his tongue hanging out. Waiting for leftovers. That was exactly what she gave him after finishing her main course elsewhere. But Ali didn't know that. So caught up in his pursuit of her, he did not see what she pursued.

At her door, he strained to catch a glimpse of her. Fiza caught him peeking and invited him in. She liked the boy more than her daughter did. Well, it was only as a could-be son-in-law that he pulled at her heart—her Pakistani heart. Now, here was a fellow Pakistani, and well behaved at that, a perfect match for her Indo-Pak daughter. Mullah, she knew was hunting for an Indian boy. She decided to strike first and directed him to her daughter who was setting up the barbecue in the garden.

'Can you help her a bit?'

Ali was beside himself at this overflow of opportunities. *Was Allah holding a sale for his followers?* Carrying his gift of chicken, he approached Zeenat on her home turf, and found her struggling with the set-up.

'I'll light it for you.'

Zeenat jumped at the sound of his voice, and then relaxed. It was only that harmless Ali. But why was he creeping up on her? And what was he offering to light?

You needed a measure of hotness to set things afire. You needed . . . yes, Shehzad is what you needed. Rock-hard and explosive!

Ali thrust forward his balti chicken in answer to her questioning look. Zeenat found this hilarious, and throwing back her head, laughed and laughed. Ali was happy to see her happy. That's all he wanted to do—be happy with her.

Zeenat let him work on the barbecue while she worked on figuring out her current status with Shehzad. They were definitely an item. She knew it. Shehzad knew it. Only they had not put a tag on it. Yet.

Adjusting the grills, Ali stole a look at her every now and then. She looked lost. But, to him she looked even lovelier when she was lost. Thankfully, Ali remained unaware as to what she was lost in. He kept worshipping her. From afar. She kept smiling at him. From afar.

It was a complicated world for sure. Zeenat's mother wanted Ali. Ali wanted Zeenat. And Zeenat wanted Shehzad. If only the moon could grant each of them their wish. Instead, it only hung up there, chuckling.

Lighting the fire, Ali turned to poetry, reciting the famous Jaun Elia's paeans.

Kitni dilkash ho tum, kitna dilju hoon main,
Kya sitam hain ki hum log mar jayenge . . .

Ghazal after ghazal came to mind when she was near. He regaled her with the ones he thought were safe and not a dead giveaway of his rising feelings.

Bahut nazdeek ati ja rahi ho,
Bicharne ka irada kar liya hain kya?

Ali was not a fast worker. He wanted to tread slowly. Surely.

But she was not sure of him. Ali was sweet. Friendly. And . . . that was it. There was not more to him than that . . . and that she was sure of!

He was still reciting something:

Pehli mulaqat thi, aur hum dono hi bebas the,
Woh zulfein nahin sambhal paaye, aur hum khudko . . .

This one had to do with her hair. Zeenat sniggered. Ali was praising her hair, that too on one of her bad-hair days! This was epic! She burst out again.

Ali mistook her laughing at him for laughing with him, and mumbled to himself, '*Dekhiye hoga yi galatfehmi, muskurana koi zaroori tha?*'

Things were really looking up for him today. It must be something to do with the stars—or the moon. Some angel up there was probably melting with kindness. He looked skywards and mumbled a thank you to no one in particular.

Zeenat was relieved to see that he had stopped singing. Poetic Ali was worse than normal Ali. His lavish praise she welcomed and enjoyed, but not this random poetry—such sing-song verses went totally over her head. They came from a world and an era she neither understood nor wanted to.

Ali, however, felt he had scored a major point with his poetry and decided to look up more verses to serenade her with in future. His wanting-to-be mother-in-law heard them in passing and patted herself for having arranged such a musical companion for her daughter. Even the moon got confused. The ways of humans defied all logic or pattern.

6

Rishi had moved on—from the pet shop that had fired him to the car showroom that hired him. Now a trainee sales assistant at Peugeot, he was supposed to sell French cars to Englishmen in London. The twenty-one-year-old Agra lad tried to whip up enthusiasm for this new profile and demonstrate all the required customer-satisfaction skills. He even dressed with care, clothing his five feet eight inches in formal pinstripes, combing his wavy, black hair neatly sideways, and pinching the freckles on his nose to make them disappear. Not that he succeeded, but the mirror told him, his square face looked quite okay for the task at hand.

Despite his best efforts, the first week itself was marred by a complaint. His superior was upset that he failed to smile while attending prospective customers. Rishi refused to fall in line and light up his face with a curve the minute someone walked in, so he was shifted to aftersales support. Once a car or part had been sold, it mattered not if the Peugeot guy smiled or looked serious.

He was expected to do well here, but Rishi was irritated. All his training in slick selling techniques was going waste. He'd invested so many hours, honing every emotional and psychological trick in the book—learning ways to catch a *bakra* the moment they walked in, then playing mind games till they zeroed in on the vehicle he wanted to sell as opposed to what they wanted to buy; next, offering multiple test drives to oblige or embarrass them into accepting an order form, and finally, exerting time-pressure tactics to close the deal as soon as possible. Rishi had graduated with honours from the company's sales training programme—only to be moved to another department that needed none of these skills.

Stuck behind a desk, he could sit unsmiling, only requiring to sound polite every time someone called or screamed on the company helpline number. Technically, he was appointed to deliver promises and delight the customer. Additionally, he was meant to replenish the busy company service workshop with parts and that's where he had his next run-in. A nasty exchange with a mechanic who was in a hurry flagged Rishi's performance and attitude again. For the second time in two weeks, he was in the red.

Rishi approached Zeenat then. She was the floor manager at the same showroom. Till now, he had mostly ignored her. But that was because she was beautiful and he had to stick to his vows. Even if she had been ugly, he would have steered clear of her. Was she not entangled with more than one of his housemates? And who knew if her thing stretched to more than one house? Rishi stopped himself with a jerk. He was on the brink of being sacked—and here he was dwelling on looks and personal affairs. His professional affairs were in dire straits right now, and when in peril in a foreign country, who would be the first person you approach? Your countryman, of course—or woman in this case. Zeenat, he recalled, had blood from both sides of the border. Appealing to her Indian haemoglobin, he made a fervent plea for help.

She did not let him down, but he did get demoted. Pushed out of the showroom if not the company, Rishi found himself stationed in the garage, supervising the pick-up and drop of cars given for test driving. This outpost had not come easily. Zeenat had to deploy a lot of charm and wile to persuade the showroom manager to retain Rishi, extolling his non-existent virtues and finding excuses for his misbehaviour when there were none. It was tiring but she was a good actor.

Rishi soon began to settle in his new role. Jangling keys and maintaining records of vehicle movement was what it mostly entailed. If there was more work he was supposed to do, he pretended to not know how to do it. And things rolled smoothly for more than a week this time.

Then he punched this white guy. Or so the white guy said. Rishi insisted he had stamped on him, and not punched him, that too accidentally. Whether it was his shoe or fist that had made contact when the vehicle was returned, it no longer mattered. That it was unintentional and totally unplanned also got ignored. What mattered was that Rishi had fallen foul of the wrong colour of skin. This was unpardonable. And so he was back on the street. And the job market. Forget Zeenat Amaan—not even someone named Katrina Kaif could have saved him this time!

Zeenat saw him again in the kitchen that night. She had come looking for Shehzad and found all the boys cooking.

At least, Ali was, and Shehzad and Rishi assisting him. They were trying to follow the chef's orders even as something tickled their insides so bad they found it hard to stand straight.

Doubling over with laughter, Shehzad chopped and peeled. Rishi fetched stuff from the fridge, recounted another slice of his sacking story that had the trio tittering again. Zeenat was struck by their teamwork. The Indian was narrating the whole tamasha, adding masala, the Bangladeshi acted it out and the Pakistani then crooned a verse in appreciation. Borders were melting and together they made merry over the overreaction of the white guy that led to the axing of the brown one.

All this tomfoolery made her livid. She had risked her reputation and position to save this scoundrel just the previous week! And he had the gall to go and screw up royally and then celebrate being fired with this comic act! The company had been right to label him their worst-ever performer. She was a fool for suspecting a racial angle. Zeenat shook her head in disgust. Rishi was a destination best avoided. She signalled Shehzad to wind up this South Asian picnic. But found him in no mood to retire yet.

So she kept waiting and watching till the boys' laughter infected her too. And pitched her right into the centre of the kitchen circus. You could see her rolling her eyes in exaggerated annoyance, like the garage supervisor must have done when the white guy reported Rishi. That brought the house down! Ali was in tears and forgot to stir his salan. Shehzad reprimanded Ali for laughing while in the line of duty. Mimicking British elegance and sophistication, he followed it up by acting out how seriously the British took even their ride in the Tube. Aping how an Englishman would not talk to anyone and walk in a straight line, even when not in a queue. And how they would make no eye contact—ever, taking special care to avoid every other person in the train or on the platform.

Rishi went to bed with a smile, forgetting he had been fired that afternoon.

7

Zeenat was on Shehzad's bed again, waiting for her Romeo to return from the studio. She wanted to surprise him. Not just with her body, but a new demand this time. He was her tenant and was therefore duty-bound to satisfy her. It's not that he did not pay his rent, but today, she wanted him to pay in kind too. And so she lay waiting.

He smelt her before he saw her—heady and tropical, reminding him of pineapple and frangipani. An audacious combination so like her! She was sprawled on his bed, her lissom length warming his sheets—and putting him in heat too. Shehzad felt all his tiredness melt away. This wild flower was so bright and energetic. She made him want to pluck her right away. But something held him back.

What was she doing in his room? She hadn't informed him before coming over and that wasn't like her! Not like them for that matter. They weren't going steady or anything.

It was an 'as-and-when-you-choose' thing they had going. He scratched his head. Were they crossing some lines here? Entering a new zone, the next level, was it? With girls, you never knew, what they think . . . what they do . . . he sure as hell didn't know.

Zeenat saw him hesitate and silently ask himself dozens of questions. She shook her head. Guys could be so dumb sometimes. When you saw a good thing, shouldn't you just grab it? Why stand there and ponder on it being there?

The Dhaka boy kept gaping like a goldfish, trying to come to terms with what he was seeing.

Zeenat sighed. This one would have to be led. So she moved. Arching up on a pillow, she looked at him and then at her pillow pointedly. The invitation in her eyes would have been hard for even a moron to miss.

He understood. Flinging his bag aside, he sauntered over to her and bent to stroke her cheek. Pushing her dark hair out of the way, he cupped her chin in his left hand and pulled her up with the other. Holding her tight against him, he brought her face up to his and looked right into her eyes.

She wrapped herself around him, liking the feel of his jeans against her skin and the metallic buttons of his jacket poking into her. His stubble grazed her cheek in a familiar way, his curls tickling her.

Shehzad was stumped. She made him gooey every time, and they had barely begun. Her softness teased the hard planes of his body. Her eyes invited every part of him to come and play, sending sexy signals till every nerve in him was talking to every nerve in her. Generating enough voltage to light up ten towns back home. 'Zeenie!' he crooned in her ear, licking the lobe after breathing up and down its folds.

And she crumbled. Her ear was her weakness and this boy knew it. She turned over, unable to take the torture any more. Her face met his lips and got bathed in one kiss after another. Going mad, she pulled him towards her, kissing him till he almost fell on top of her.

A jumble of hands and feet and hair they were, clothed and yet on fire. Her skirt and his jeans were no wall. They patted and pinched and squeezed each other through the fabric, in no hurry to undress. It was a little later that his shirt landed on the floor, followed by her dress. His bared eagle tattoo now perched on her bra cups, driving her insane. She stroked its wings, kissed the head of the bird and blew on it—hot and feathery.

Shehzad shivered. She would kill him one day with her touch—he was sure of it.

'Mine . . .'

'What?' He did not quite catch what she was saying. Too much was happening to him right now. How could he concentrate on words?

'Not you,' she muttered, still caressing his tattoo. 'I was telling this bird something.'

'Bird?' Shehzad saw her fingering his eagle with such tenderness that he felt jealous and remarked, 'You're more into my tattoo than me!'

Zeenat was thrilled to see him go green and knew that it was time to ask him what she wanted.

'I'll leave your bird only if you . . .'

What was her game? He had no clue.

'If you give me a bird of my own.'

Her words zapped him. Did she really mean it? No. She couldn't. No. Why would she?

Shehzad kept staring at her, unsure of what was happening.

Zeenat cupped his face. 'Yes,' she said, 'Yes.'

He looked at her in wonder, not believing what she had just said.

'Ink me, Shehzad!' she said in a husky voice. 'Ink me. Now.'

Gathering her in a tight hug, he asked, 'Why?'

Zeenat shrugged it off.

'Okay, we'll do it some time soon,' he promised and moved to unhook her bra. He couldn't wait any longer.

She shoved his hand away and said, 'Now. I want it now. First.'

'Zeenie . . .' Shehzad was surprised but hoped she would understand that he wanted her so badly!

But she was stubborn. And so there he was, bending over her with his tattoo gun, etching a butterfly on her shoulder.

'Make her big and beautiful,' Zeenat ordered as he worked. 'I want her to fly far.'

Shehzad was engrossed in his art. Her body was his canvas today. A fluttery creature he would gift her. A tall beauty, with delicate, iridescent wings. Lost in his artwork, he had gone quiet.

Zeenat kept up her chatter. 'My butterfly will roam the world. Far and wide it will go.'

He said nothing.

'Next, I'll get a parachute.'

He was shading the wings and muttered, 'Hmm . . .'

'On my arm . . . a chute on my left arm.'

The left wing was done and he turned to the right one now.

'Then I want a plane . . .'

His hand stilled. The gun kept pushing the ink down that point.

'I'll take off in my plane . . . telling no one . . .'

A shiver went up his body, knifing him, shaking the hand that gripped the tattoo gun, and spreading the ink past the wing.

'I'll go wher . . .'

'Stop!' He screamed and flung the tattoo gun on the bed and shut his ears with both hands.

'Ouch!' The needle had pricked her shoulder before the gun was suddenly whisked off. Feeling uncomfortable, she held up her arm and examined her left shoulder. The design had smudged! Her tattoo . . . spoilt . . . the ink creeping beyond the outline.

Zeenat lost it then. 'You bastard . . . I'll kill you!'

Shehzad had left the bed and stood facing the wall, pummelling it. She got off it too and marched up to him. She was seething.

'Don't hide your face, you asshole!' she shrieked and tried to turn him around.

But he threw her off. Hurt and shaking with anger, she caught him again and screamed, 'You bloody messed it up . . . I'll make you pay . . . I . . . I'll . . .'

Shehzad turned around suddenly and shut her up with a finger on his lips. His eyes were wild, she saw. And glazed. His face contorted with pain. His breath came too fast and he was clearly on edge.

She did a double take. What the hell! Why was he mad? First, he fucked up her tattoo. Now this . . .

'Shehzad . . .'

He clamped her mouth with his hand and said, 'Can't you see, bitch . . . can't you see? I'm in pain!'

Zeenat twisted and shook his hand off. 'I don't care! Just don't touch me again, you loser.' And she turned to pick up her dress.

'Yeah, right, you bitches never care . . .'

As she stormed out his door, she heard him scream, 'No . . . you only play . . .'

Her shoulder was bleeding a bit, her heart however was bleeding even more. But surely not more than his. For, his wound was old—very old—festering since she'd flown off in a plane, abandoning him and his dad. Years ago. His mom. Yes, in a plane. And now, his girl too wanted a plane . . . a plane for a tattoo.

'Bitches! All of them. Bitches!'

8

The ethos of hard work and enterprise was something Rishi never wanted to cultivate. All his energy went in getting over past baggage and ensuring things never got that way again. Basic survival was his only ambition. He wanted to reach a point where he could just about manage, without rising, without shining. His unpolished talent and limited devotion to duty worked well with this micro goal. It was in low-profile and less taxing positions that he actually thrived. Right now, however, he was on the road, stripped of work and pay. Being fired had definitely not been on his agenda. Yet, he took it in the best of spirits and decided to move on.

The first day without work felt awesome. The second day dragged. By the fourth morning, however, he got antsy and searched frantically for the right opening. The job boards were overflowing with postings. But unfortunately, nothing remotely matching his medium qualifications was up for grabs.

Rishi scanned the listings morning, noon and night, hoping for a happy hour that would bring good tidings. But all he hit was a zero.

Wasn't there something I could do? Something . . . anything . . .

No, he didn't want to serve tables. Neither could he solicit business on the streets. Not that he didn't look good, but only that he wasn't that confident—at least not now. Delivering stuff was again not up his sleeve. He was prone to knocking at the wrong door. As for entertaining, Rishi would be the last guy hired for such an engaging purpose. That left only sales. And he had flunked in both his recent assignments. It looked like he was destined to spend the rest of his days in England, playing the pensive role of a hungry, jobless immigrant, unwanted by the state that allowed him to stay and as well as the state that let him fly off.

Those who knew Rishi explained that he was scarred. But scars either make people better or bitter. With Rishi, one could never tell for sure. When asked—usually at a job interview— he always described himself as a 'work-in-progress'. If probed, he would elaborate that he was a slow learner, but a learner nevertheless. The goals he listed were unconventional too. He only wanted a salary that allowed him to eat, drink and exist. Period. How about getting his meals in the Southall gurdwara langars then, suggested someone. But that would cramp his style, he argued.

Rishi did not believe that he was going downhill professionally; it was the employers who were getting more exacting in what they wanted. They listed out extremely specific technical requirements, and needed you to demonstrate skills quickly. Rishi was definitely not cut out for such things. But like every dog has his day, Rishi had his too. One on which he stumbled on the perfect job ad. It required no major qualification other than being a desi and having some experience in sales. Rishi was hired immediately. His job was to chat up rich desi babas and convince them to buy ad space in *Desi Beats,* the paper that was literally the heartbeat of the Indian population in England.

Rishi was thrilled to have landed this average paying and non-demanding job, that too in an office which was a veritable Asia in London. He sighted a Lankan and a lady from Karachi, another from Cambodia or Kuala Lumpur, he couldn't be sure. Booming over them were the Gujaratis and the Punjabis. It was chaotic and homely. Not that he was homesick, but this was familiar territory and he felt safe.

Getting hired can be a tiring thing. Rishi reported to meet the team but postponed the launch of his new career till the next morning, citing pending stuff he needed to clear. Actually, it was his head he wanted to air out; he wanted to idle away one last evening before returning to the grind of a schedule. His wish was granted. With a singing heart and dancing eyes, he stepped back into the house and greeted Shehzad cheerily, almost shocking the Bangladeshi to the point of heart failure.

His housemate shook him to ascertain that he was real. Rishi laughed.

'Got exchanged, did you?'

Rishi winked in answer. Shehzad was sure he was hallucinating. The Indian had gotten drunk or had hit his head. Or maybe, this was a phoney. This couldn't be Rishi. Not their Rishi. Definitely not that morose, keeping-to-himself damp squib he had been living with for months. Before the Bangladeshi seriously lost his marbles, Rishi explained the reason for his good cheer.

'I got a new job. Exactly the sort I wanted.'

Shehzad stared open-mouthed. What the Indian was saying made no sense to him, but he let it go. At least, the bugger was smiling and talking tonight. Most of the time, he reminded Shehzad of that grave and gloomy Indian PM, the one who was never audible on TV, even with a battery of mikes facing him. Thankfully, his government had been replaced—such a yawn he was. Shaking his head, Shehzad got up to raid the fridge. So much confusion wasn't good for his stomach. He needed to fuel up, eat something hot and spicy to get his mind ticking again.

Rishi stretched out comfortably on the sofa and decided to doze off. But a shout from the kitchen messed up his plan. The Dhaka boy needed help. What Rishi could make out in his half-asleep state was that Shehzad was succumbing to hunger, having found nothing palatable in the fridge to feed on.

This was a desperate situation. Everyone knew of Shehzad and his starvation bouts. He went totally crazy when hunger pangs hit him and food was not at hand. Ali usually cooked extra food and stocked leftovers just for such emergencies. The famished Bangladeshi had thus attacked the fridge with much hope. But found only milk or stuff that needed to be prepared. As cooking was something he couldn't do alone, the new-and-improved Rishi had to be summoned.

Shehzad lined up three options from the stuff in the fridge. Together, they could surely manage to whip up one out of the three. But where was the Agra boy? How long it took to move his ass from the hall to the kitchen! And why didn't he answer? Had he gone mute again, like his ex-PM? The Bangla stomach was growling loud and making him really impatient, so he went to investigate. The Indian was checking something on his phone. Shehzad wanted to wring his neck and then feast on his sullen meat to wreak revenge. But even that would involve cooking, something he couldn't manage by himself. So he held his instincts in check and settled on verbal abuse.

Scanning cheap takeaway options on his phone, Rishi did not see Shehzad coming. Something cold suddenly whizzed past his ears, making him jump, and his phone went flying. He turned around to see what had hit him—and stared into a jar of pickles! It was *his* pickle jar! That vile Bangladeshi vermin charged into Rishi again, attacking him with Indian pickle, along with every fucking abuse known in the subcontinent.

Rishi screamed, 'Chill, man! Chill!'

But his starved and simmering housemate was not in the frame of mind to listen. Rishi then picked up his phone and waved it in front of the Dhaka storm like a white flag. 'See! See, what I was doing,' he tried to shout above the tornado raging and swearing full blast. 'I was looking at meal deals— my treat.'

Shehzad stopped then, liking what he had just heard. Ordering was always easier than cooking, and if someone else was paying, he could wait.

9

All that going up and down restaurant options, and calculation after calculation to arrive at the place from which they could extract the most after shelling out the least, brought them in the end to one place. Nawab Balti—Ali's restaurant. They decided to land up around twelve to avail the two-for-one offer. After midnight, you could eat anything there at half-price. That suited them the best. Also, Ali could take care of extras, if there were any, and possibly throw in a free dessert too.

So hands in pockets, earphones plugged in, the two reached Whitechapel on the Tube. Shehzad felt nostalgic each time he set foot here—this was Bangla town! But he was careful not to show it. He acted like a Londoni—born and brought up in England—distinguished from the visa dependent riff-raff crawling all around. Rishi got caught up in the smells and sales that were a trademark of this East London street. Cheap buys tempted him at every corner. He liked checking out the T-shirts and belts, looking for the impossible bargain. Shehzad joined him in his search.

'These are shirts . . . T-shirts,' Rishi pointed out.

'Yeah. So?'

'Why you looking? You almost never wear one.'

Shehzad looked to check if his housemate had suddenly gone insane and found him grinning wickedly. Now, what was this? Twice in one day, the Indian actually looked happy. Life was such a puzzle. It fried his brains.

'Salmanbhai, how's this black one?' Rishi turned to Shehzad and asked, with a laugh.

The Londoni eyed the Indian warily as he held up a T-shirt for inspection.

'Not for you.'

Rishi was wise enough to not ask why. He had no desire to be butchered in public. Shehzad had exacted suitable revenge for that shirtless Salman Khan jibe. The two then walked slowly towards their destination, letting the clock roll towards midnight. Shehzad paused to admire the striking street art. Turning to his companion, he explained why the painted crane was a notch above the masterpieces displayed in western museums.

'This one comes from the heart . . . not the brush.'

Rishi was filled with a new respect for his housemate. Shehzad was clearly not as dumb as he acted. His eye for visual detail and artistic merit had escaped him till now. They wound their way past the waiters hawking for business. 'Free snack . . . come in . . . free snack . . .' This was normal in Brick Lane, a speciality of the area, in fact. All these deals, however, could not match the deal they would wrangle out of their Ali.

Nawab Balti! They had reached their desired destination. The duo sauntered in, cocky and smiling.

Attending to a customer, Ali happened to look up and was startled. What were these *tharkis*, these good-for-nothings doing here? Had something gone wrong? *Allah rehmat kare . . .* he prayed and bounced up to them at once.

Shehzad motioned to Rishi not to reveal why they had come. He wanted to fool around with Ali a bit before sitting down to eat.

When Ali looked at them questioningly, Shehzad asked, 'You caught the news, did you?'

'*Kya?*'

'The high commission in Islamabad was attacked. They're rounding up all the Pakis here.'

Ali went white. Shehzad leaned close and whispered in his ear, 'They're cancelling all visas.'

Ali looked at Rishi. The Indian was enjoying this attack across the border way too much. The chef collapsed on to the nearest chair, sweating. People were wearing jackets but he felt like he was in Lahore in June. Rishi and Shehzad pulled up chairs and joined him on the table. The Bangladeshi pulled out the menu stuck on the centrepiece and began reading it out loud. Rishi fought on which dish to order first. Ali stared at the jokers occupying his table and suddenly things began to get clear. The bastards were freaking him out on his visa-fright syndrome! They were chopping him up, that too in his own restaurant.

He got up to throw them out. There was still an hour or two of business left. He couldn't handle work with these clowns at his elbow.

'Out, you two! Out!' He barked, his suave persona forgotten for once. But it was as if he had not said anything.

The two failed to react one inch. They went on debating their options and figuring out the sequence in which to have them.

'Dahibhalla first or at the end?'

'I want to end with kulfi falooda.'

Ali was fast losing every ounce of his legendary patience. These inhuman louts didn't deserve any. Yet, he held back. This was, after all, his workplace. He couldn't explode even if he had every goddamn reason to. 'Leave,' he hissed, looking the two idiots in the eye.

'Relax. It's not good for your blood pressure.'

Ali vowed that one day he would kill this Bangladeshi— this scoundrel who pretended to be a Londoni. Plunge him down his Farakka Barrage.

'We're celebrating!'

Celebrating? What? Why? Ali was lost. But he refrained from asking. Who knew, this might just be another prank.

'Rishi's got a new job!'

Ali looked at the Indian to confirm. And saw his eyes twinkling happily. The Pakistani's heart melted at this visual confirmation. Holding out his giant, hairy hand, he congratulated his housemate with a hearty handshake and then finding this to be less, hauled him out of his chair and hugged him.

Shehzad whistled. 'Now for the treat.'

Ali eyed the Bangladeshi, unsure of what he was implying. He could sure feed his housemates but he would have to pay. He couldn't dole out freebies—this wasn't his restaurant. If this was Lahore, then they could come any time!

'Rishi's treating!'

Rishi confirmed and asked Ali to decide what the three of them should eat. 'We'll wait till the clock strikes the witching hour though!'

Ali laughed at his deal-hungry housemates. It was good to have them here—it felt somewhat like home. He returned to the kitchen with a smile, his brain listing out the dishes and the order in which he would have them served at the table. Yes, tonight would be a feast

It was half-past twelve. The restaurant was now almost empty. The few people inside, like the housemates, had walked in late to eat at half-price. A sprinkling of customers who would pay the full price too lingered. Ali now joined his friends at the table. The duo were stuffing themselves like it was their last supper, a supper for which they did not have to chop, peel, stir or stew anything. They finished off his signature dishes at a speed that was breakneck.

'Stop!' Ali told the gluttons. 'Or you'll burst!'

They ignored him and continued to gorge on the delicacies.

'You won't understand,' Shehzad explained after polishing off the dal. 'You got food around you all the time.'

'I cook, don't eat it.'

'Same thing!' Shehzad had his own warped logic. 'You can see it, smell it, taste it whenever you want.'

Ali shook his head. He was an ass to argue with these asses. Pointless talking to them, it was better to stuff his mouth like the other two. After all, Rishi was treating.

Tummies full, the three returned home singing. First, Rishi crooned a Salman Khan number—an ode to his frequently shirtless housemate. Shehzad followed it up with a Honey Singh chartbuster that had them dancing on the street. Back at home, it was time for Ali's *shayri*—Jaun Elia, Ali's favourite. He crooned at the door:

Aaj bahut din baad mein apne kamre tak aa nikla tha,
Jun hi darwaaza khola hai, uski khushboo aayi hai.

Rishi whistled and clapped. 'Wah, wah!'
Tum jab aogi toh khoya hua paogi mujhe,
Meri tanhaayi mein khwaabonke siva kuch bhi nahi.
Mere kamre ko sajane ki tamanna hai tujhe,
Mere kamre mein kitabon ki siva kuch nahi . . .
Shehzad immediately wanted to know who Ali was reciting all of these verses for.

'*Tum bhi chup hai, main bhi chup hoon . . .*' Ali returned with a smile.

10

Meanwhile, thousands of miles away, life was no longer merry. No hustle and bustle of cars driving in, of people walking in to order food. There were no children shrieking and running around, and no mothers stopping them. No Bollywood music blaring in the background. No diners trying to shout their order over all the noise. Not even waiters chasing the cooks to rush their orders, or customers bickering over their bills. And no groups of people jumping in to take the table that had just been vacated.

The dhaba was no longer a dhaba. It was bereft of people, food, and life. Only the signboard still hung, lonely and irrelevant, presiding over a downed shutter. The board said Haji's Hotel in bright yellow but there was no one around to read it. Behind the shutter, once Lahori thaals and nihari were prepared. Order after order for biryani had to be met in a piping rush. Today, tables and chairs stood stacked up and dusty in a corner. There wasn't a whiff of smoke or smell of things cooking.

Wasim Sahib was the only one who came here now. He would stand outside and stare at the locked-up place for an hour every day. But lately, even he had stopped coming— he couldn't. Things were disintegrating fast, even home was no longer home. His family lived at his place but without him. They came hounding him day and night, every day, demanding the same thing, till he was no longer there for them to come after. Only the family was left to tell them they knew not where he was.

And that's what they told Ali too when he had called in the morning. He had been calling and asking for Abbu every day, and every day, they fobbed him off with excuses like they fobbed off the loan recovery agents. Only the excuse they gave their son was different from the one they gave the bank. But today, the family finally told Ali what they told the bank agents every day. Abbu was gone.

Ali went numb. He couldn't believe things had come to this. Abbu had left home. Left Ammi. And he was just sitting here. Cooking lamb chops. He banged his head against the wall, crying, but shedding no tears. He was cracking up inside, grieving about not being in Lahore.

Thousands of miles away, Ammi could sense he was not okay. She called to stop him from breaking, confiding that Abbu was well wherever he was and that Ali should not waste away worrying; rather, he should keep doing what he set out to do because now more than ever, the family's hopes were riding on their boy in London. Ali took heart that at least Ammi was in touch with Abbu. Holding on to that ray, he resolved to get tougher and prepared himself to win.

Rishi and Shehzad, in adjacent rooms, remained oblivious to these developments till the Partition topic came up in the kitchen that night, and burnt the bhindi frying in the pan. One thing led to another and the whole dhaba story burst out. Trust the Bangladeshi to pick on the past to screw up the present. He began by taunting Ali when the chef yelled at him for messing up the kitchen counter. 'This is just a countertop. You guys fucked my whole country with all your East Pakistan shit.'

'Shehu . . .' warned Ali, wanting to slice off the Dhakaite's tongue.

'For once, you're right,' Rishi chipped in, patting Shehzad's back.

'Good, we cut loose,' the Bangladeshi declared, playing with the onion skins on the chopping board.

'And how did that help?' Ali came to stand behind him and nearly yelled into his ear. 'What you got today? A delta, Runa Laila and . . . ?'

Shehzad turned to Ali in anger. Rishi left the rice he was soaking and wedged himself between his taller housemates.

'Guys, chill . . .'

'You tell me what you got first . . .' Shehzad screamed over Rishi's head.

'Kalashnikovs!' Rishi whispered in the Bangladeshi's ear and Ali heard him.

'Yeah, like your Nehru didn't go pandering to the Soviets, no?'

'We don't live on foreign aid like you,' Rishi hit back. 'Fighting others' wars.'

The Pakistani swung the Indian to face him and looked him in the eye. 'You still can't get over the fact that we broke away, can you? Partition goes on hurting.'

'Dream on . . .' taunted the Indian, raising his neighbour's blood pressure.

'Look . . .' Shehzad now tried to cool his seething housemates, scared that things might boil out of control. With an India–Pakistan situation, you can never tell. 'Let's sit and discuss this over dinner. Like civilized humans . . . please?'

In all this brouhaha, the bhindi in the pan went from green to brown, irritating Ali even further. 'These Indians, they spoil everything . . . *hamara naam . . . kaam . . . qabiliyat . . .* everything.'

'Blame your debts on us too—go on!' Rishi goaded, despite Shehzad trying to pull him away from the kitchen.

Discarding the burnt vegetable in the bin, Ali let loose.

'Yes, everything! You Indians wrecked everything for Pakistan. Leaving us with nothing after Partition. Killing our people, taking away our institutions, our towns, industry, water—everything!'

'Everything?'

'Yes, everything! We had to build everything from scratch. You . . . you were making us pay for not living the Hindu way. And we're still paying. I'm paying. My Abbu's paying. Our dhaba is paying. All for you Hindus!'

The Pakistani was blabbering now. The other two had riled him no end. First, the Dhaka fellow with his smart-arse comments and then the Indian backing him up. And blackening his bhindi too! Especially when there was so much on his mind. Insensitive idiots! They just didn't know where to draw the line!

'Tell me one thing,' Rishi began again, at the dining table. Shehzad had herded them there, along with the remaining dinner, hoping that the dal and rotis would keep their mouths busy and save him more Partition noise.

'How is Partition affecting you, your Abbu, and your dhaba today?'

'You ruined our economy . . . the reason why we're swimming in debt today. Paying and repaying loans.'

'Not us. Your bloody dictators did you in. The honour goes to them.'

Shehzad couldn't stop himself from butting in. 'He's right. That Ayub and Yahya Khan—they tried the same stunt in East Pakistan too. Dictating. Trying to control everything—even our language.'

'And what ruin are you talking of?' Rishi said to Ali. 'All that fertile land you got in Punjab, that too fully irrigated.'

'Cotton and jute too,' piped in the Bangladeshi.

Ali got mad at this dual attack. 'Siding with India won't help you. They screw everyone,' the Pakistani informed the Bangladeshi. 'And you, Rishi—you guys are always creating trouble, eating up whatever we got. Because of you, our defence spending's spiked ten times, leaving nothing for honest, simple folk. No wonder, Abbu had to go.' His voice shook now. 'Leave our home . . . our dhaba . . . all gone . . .'

Not understanding where all of this was coming from, Rishi, in a fit of rage, pushed his chair back, picked up his plate and took off to his room, telling Ali that he didn't want to see or hear him again.

Shehzad put out a hand to comfort Ali. The usually polite man was staring down his plate and still shaking with emotion. He was not one for such drama. Other than cricket and Jaun Elia, not much ruffled Ali's feathers. And what was that he said about his Abbu? About his leaving home? And their dhaba? Shehzad would have to figure a delicate way to get that story out. The guy was all messed up now. In fact, their whole house was. He shouldn't have started this. Fuck!

For at least a week now, he would have to spread peace and act like—what was the name of that Tibetan monk in India? Ah yes, the Dalai Lama.

11

Rishi, Shehzad and Ali walked down George Street to their landlord's in complete silence. The Indian and the Pakistani had been operating in 'talk-only-when-absolutely-necessary' mode ever since the Partition fiasco. Shehzad was wondering what the hell he would do at Zeenat's place when he was mad at her and she with him. Yet, here they were, marching up together to her place.

Actually, Mullah had called. And when your landlord summons, you have to go. Even if it was to attend the birthday of someone you don't really care about. At least, that's how Rishi saw it. Shehzad's case was different. He didn't want to go because he was getting too caught up with her and that was not his scene. She too was still hung up about the tattoo botch-up. But there was no way he could explain this complicated tale to Mullah. Ali went armed with sweet and spongy rasmalai and a smile that he would unleash only at her door. It was an honour to be invited to spend this special day with her. And he had effusively said the same to her father. How lucky he was to have Mullah as his landlord!

Fiza received them at the door. Gushing over Ali and his rasmalai, she took him to Zeenat, signalling the other two to follow. Rishi had written 'Happy Birthday' on a card and Shehzad had got a bottle, hoping it would add some sparkle to the night.

Zeenat was all dolled up for the occasion in a sheer mauve shirt and a slinky blue skirt and navy pumps. Shiny silver studs and a bracelet added to her glow. Her hair was clasped in a clip at her left shoulder. She had clearly dressed with care but acted like it was no big deal. And going more dramatic, she rebuked Mullah twice for bothering the boys for such a non-event. Aware of her penchant for drama, no one took her seriously. The elders looked on dreamily at their wonderful daughter, catching the smile in her eyes when the boys walked in.

For reasons unknown, their daughter wanted to keep her pleasure at their arrival under wraps, so they played along. Her offhand demeanour soon began to rankle Shehzad and Rishi. So, after handing over the bottle and the card, they proceeded to lavish all their attention on the canapés and kebabs piled high on the table. This further aggravated the princess's unholy temper. Oblivious to the undercurrents, Ali played both guest and host, moving around with the tray, serving with a glowing heart. His chatter warmed Zeenat's parents more than the fire lit for the occasion.

Zeenat preened and strutted in her heels, looking more appetizing than the fare on the table. But Rishi kept his eyes glued to his phone and Shehzad pretended to be unmoved. Things got moving only after Fiza elbowed her husband to get up and let the children be. The awkwardness in the hall was not of their making, but they had no clue. Ali was the only one who cashed in on their departure. He began his own version of Coke Studio a la Jaun Elia, paying his ode to the birthday girl in ecstatic poetry:

Ajab ek shor sa bar pa hai kahin
Koi khaamosh hoga ya hai kahin

Hai kuchh hai saki jaise ye sab kuchh
Ab se pehle bhi ho chukka hai kahin

Har bar mere saamnay aati rahi ho tum
Har bar tum se mil ke bicharta raha hun mein

Tum kaun ho ye khud bhi nahin jaanti ho tum
Mein kaun hun ye khud bhi nahi jaanta humein.

The magic of the words changed the mood of the party. Rishi, Shehzad and Zeenat were drawn into a beautiful world of romance and laughter and merriment. The birthday girl cast off her nonchalant attitude and embraced the boys anew, for the night was young and it would be criminal to waste another minute pandering to her fast-fading anger.

A change of mood called for a change in music. Zeenie cast off her shoes and put on some thumping techno music. 'Let's party!' she declared.

That was the cue for Shehzad to bring out the bottles from their hiding place beneath the console. She didn't have to tell him they were there. His eyes and nose had zoomed in on these party vitals within minutes of entering. They had been stashed there for a purpose, and he had figured that out instantly.

Dimming the lights and crowding round the table, the foursome got merry even before the champagne was popped. Ali and Rishi were still not talking to each other, but when there was food, music and alcohol, one did not necessarily need conversation to enjoy oneself. To Shehzad went the honour of uncorking the bottle and the first toast. 'To the yummiest heroine of tomorrow! The sexy and sizzling Zeenie!'

The boys whistled and clapped. Zeenat hugged him then, gathering Shehzad close and not wanting to let go.

'To the dreamiest lady in London!' Ali pronounced with stars in his eyes. She rewarded him with a kiss on the nose.

Rishi was inaudible as always.

Mullah and his wife heard the volume go up and slipped content into their sheets, glad that their princess was finally having a good time. These last few days, she had been moping and not quite been her normal self. Unaware of her spat with Shehzad, they had invited the tenants over to cheer up their solitary flower. These boys had been dominating her conversations at home, so Mullah deduced they would be his best bet to make the birthday a success. As always, he was right.

The night was high on Bollywood numbers. Ali knew what Zeenat liked, and he played one hit after another. Even Rishi was on the floor, unable to resist the catchy beat. The music took him back to Agra and Delhi . . . and to those loud, sultry nights awash with *daaru* and dance. Ali knew every word of every song by heart and sang noisily as he jumped and twisted all over the floor. His energy got the night kicking on the right note.

Shehzad fooled around with the bottle he had brought. Drinking from it, dancing with it hanging from his mouth, taking another swig, swaying, pouring it down Zeenie's mouth and neck, and then down his own, all the time dancing. Zeenat danced like the floor was begging her to play with it. *Tuk tuk tuk ardi . . . Ghitpit tuk ardi . . . Poora London thum akda!* With her endless energy, her contagious excitement, she was gyrating like there was no tomorrow. She wooed the room with her *thumka*s, *jhatka*s and *latka*s, her bindaas frolic on the floor making her the Helen of every male heart in the vicinity. Shehzad brushed against her. Ali enveloped her in a bear hug and swayed. Rishi joined his mates in circling her, whooping and shaking.

Empty bottles rolled on the floor. Rishi had hit his limit. Shehzad didn't have any. Zeenat had upped hers. Even Ali had more than his usual amount. The night got high, and guards were lowered. Zeenat was swinging alone on the floor now. The boys parked themselves around her—on the floor, sofa and cushion—feasting their eyes on her. She swayed and teased, her moves growing bolder and more exaggerated. Bending on to a chair, the birthday girl flaunted the arch in her back. Ali forgot to blink. *'Aisi hoon laila . . . har koi chahe mujhse milna akela'.* The song said what the boys couldn't.

The liquor sure was loosening things up. Coming up to where Ali sat open-mouthed, she smiled, turned around and shook her hips in his face. Shehzad lay watching, propped against the leg of the settee. He was dying to pull her over but held back. And then she got down on all fours and approached him, crawling sexily. She surprised him by rubbing her booty on him, allowing him to touch and explore. Looking him in the eye, and then moving off with a laugh.

The song ended, and it was more than what Ali could take in a night. He decided to leave while he was still in a position to. Shehzad did not respond when Ali checked if he was ready to leave. As for Rishi, even in his inebriated state, Ali was loathe to speak to him. So he trundled off, after a goodbye hug which did not quite register with Zeenat, for her attention was elsewhere.

Shehzad was singing in her blood, her nerves—in every inch of her. And then he was on her. Taking her on the cushion. On the floor. They were a tangle of hands and legs, half-awake but demanding. Hungry.

Hunger was what had driven Rishi to the kitchen. He was looking for the platter of nibbles Madam Mullah had served earlier. Liquor always whetted his appetite and it had been a long night. He never meant it to be this way, but what the heck, he was not drunk for sure. There was no risk of a hangover on day one of his new job. Food would clear the slight fuzziness hanging around him. Finding the galouti kebab, he attacked it with gusto, stuffing his face till every inch of his tongue and tummy were satisfied.

Satiated, Shehzad fell back. She always felt better than last time. But was that logical? His head was too woozy to answer. Suddenly he started feeling cold. And queasy. Where was the loo? He had to make it there! Stumbling, he somehow reached the bathroom. He shut the door and was bending to puke when he hit the floor, passing out.

Rishi returned to a hall filled with smoke and the smell of alcohol and the birthday girl sprawled senseless on the floor. Shehzad was nowhere around. Gathering her in his arms, Rishi fumbled as he put her open top together and whisked her hair out of the way. Swearing, he carried her up to her bed. Depositing the body plastered to him on to the mattress, he covered her up with a sheet and raced out. Such closeness to such beauty defied every clause in his promises to himself. That wasn't acceptable. Never.

12

Zeenat got up with surprisingly not as big a hangover as she had feared. The left part of her head throbbed and even the weak sunlight streaming into the room made her squint. Beyond that, the rest of her functioned more or less okay. Sizing herself up in the mirror, she couldn't miss the afterglow of last night's party. Despite the crinkled blouse and skirt of yesterday, she looked like a million pounds, vouched the mirror. It was all Shehzad's doing! She was eighteen today. And he had kissed her in eighteen erotic parts in celebration. Aah! Her head hurt and was a bit foggy. Some juice would help clear it. She wanted to rewind every minute of last night, especially the ending.

What was this other thing her mirror was showing up today? A note! Stuck on the mirror with tape. Just like the notes she used to leave tacked all over the house for her parents to discover every time she went camping. How cute! With a nostalgic smile, she removed it and read it aloud. It was longer than she had thought. A letter, not a note! It took her a while to finish, a long while. They had been wanting to tell her this when she turned eighteen. Her head was going fuzzy again. Zeenat scrunched the letter up and shoved it in the drawer and went off to sleep again. She didn't want to get up for a long, long time.

By afternoon, she was at house number 104. The place felt like home. Ali was cleaning his shoes. Shehzad had taken the day off from the studio. His mind was still too plastered to do any inking. A pot of something was boiling in the kitchen. Zeenat hung around, inhaling the familiar scene. Her eyes were on all of them, and she spoke non-stop. To Ali. To Shehzad. And even to Rishi who had come back early. His first day at work had been a cakewalk.

She was on a different plane today. Rishi sensed it the minute he walked in. She confirmed it by including him in her conversations. He had no choice but to reply. He still avoided Ali though. Things were still frigid between those two nations in this house. But not for long. Zeenat squashed the boys together on the sofa and forced them to join hands like scouts in some weird cult. And then made them promise to let go of any ill will towards each other.

'You guys gave me the best start to my year,' she told them. 'I need the three of you together. Always.'

Rishi looked up at her, incredulous. Shehzad asked if she had got drunk again today. Ali sat impassive. Her eyes showed that she meant it. Ali puffed out his chest magnanimously and was the first to stand up. Turning to Rishi, he hoisted him up and into his arms. Shehzad clapped from his perch and in a second, the tensions of the last few weeks melted away. The house was one again—an undivided, mad house!

Half an hour later, Ali's cell phone rang, intruding into their all-important round-table conference. Ali, Rishi, Shehzad and Zeenat were talking about what to cook for dinner, wanting to get it out of the way before Ali left for the restaurant. The Pakistani frowned when he saw the number. *They never call at this hour! I've already spoken to them twice this morning.*

'Pick it up, man,' Shehzad growled.

Ali did so with more than a little trepidation.

The rest continued to fight over whether to make paneer lababdar or chicken tikka. Rishi swore by his paneer whereas Zeenat and Shehzad were chicken crazies. The deciding vote would go to Ali for he was the one who would actually cook it.

'Ali!' All three yelled at once.

He stood leaning against the wall, the handset stuck to his ear, saying nothing. It didn't seem like he was listening, neither to them nor to whosoever was on the phone.

'Janaab,' said Zeenat, 'too late to be hungover now. Get to work!'

Rishi's sixth sense sent him rushing up to his friend. With a jerk, he took the handset from Ali and saw, as he had suspected, that the line was dead. His friend was not on the phone but in another zone, and not a happy one at that. Guiding him to the sofa, Rishi signalled the other two to come over.

'Abbu!' Ali cried out to the three pairs of eyes inspecting him with visible concern.

He didn't need to tell them Abbu was gone. They knew this time that he was gone for good. Rishi held him and cried silently. Shehzad grabbed his shoulder and tried to squeeze the pain away. Zeenat prayed for the departed soul.

Ali sat numb, letting his new family minister him. But a barrage of calls from Lahore forced him to reclaim his senses and think on his feet. There were the funeral arrangements to discuss and the expenses to calculate, along with figuring out possible funds for the ceremony. Even lists of relatives to inform had to be drawn up, so Ali got busy.

There was too much consuming his mind, leaving little space and time to dwell on the departed soul. Even death, Rishi concluded, was getting to be more a function of practicality than emotion now. So cold-blooded and businesslike! A shiver crept up his spine.

Zeenat entered Ali's room to help him pack and did a double take. It looked anything but Ali's room. Kurtas were spread all over the bed. Shirts and pants were flung on the chair. The floor was littered with books and paper. She almost tripped over the strap of a bag lying near the door. And Ali? Where was he? She found him crouched in a corner, his head buried in his hands. Zeenat knelt by him and raised his head. His eyes were glazed.

In answer to Zeenat's unspoken question, he thrust his green passport forward. His hands were quivering.

She didn't understand. And he was in no position to explain. She called for the boys then. They all crowded into that corner, trying to make sense of what was happening to Ali now.

'Shit!'

That was Rishi. He had been looking at Ali's passport up and down, trying to figure what could've gone wrong now. 'You can't go back, bro?' Actually, it was more a statement than a question.

The Pakistani wept at this, confirming what Rishi had deduced.

Shehzad punched the wall. He was angry, frustrated. And wanted to destroy this dictatorial visa regime and its suffocating restrictions. Bloody discriminating pigs!

'I'll lend it to you,' Zeenat offered her grieving friend, misunderstanding his problem.

'No, Zeenie. No,' Shehzad barked. 'It's not that.' He was too irritated to elaborate further.

She turned to Rishi who was helping Ali on to the chair. 'With his work permit,' Rishi explained, 're-entry can be a problem if he takes off,'

'Even for a death in the family?' Zeenat asked in disbelief

'Even for a death,' Rishi told her.

She left after a while. There was nothing for her to do. Not even packing. No one was going anywhere. Shehzad persuaded Ali to go out with him to pray. Visiting Allah at least was not yet controlled by the Entry Clearance Officers.

The house had gone dead quiet. Rishi sat by himself, unable to get over Ali's stricken face. He'd come to England for his Abbu. Only for him. And now, he couldn't go back to him—even this one last time. Life was such a bitch! He was no less. Rishi cursed himself. How he'd fought the fellow over something that happened seventy-plus years ago? Before either of them even existed? He swore, hating himself. Got up, paced around the room, tried to calm down . . . all the time itching to lessen his friend's pain in some way—any way.

And then he had the most brilliant idea. Rishi re-entered Ali's room and picked up the books that Zeenat had stacked on the desk. It wasn't there. He tried the cupboard next, and found it in the drawer. Abbu's book of recipes. It contained his treasured balti chicken recipe. It was Ali's heartbeat. Rishi read it once . . . twice . . . and thrice. Yes, he could make it. He had to. He had to bring the smile back on his friend's face.

It was late evening by the time Ali and Shehzad came back. Ali was not hungry, and even Shehzad's stomach was surprisingly not growling tonight. But the balti chicken changed all that. The surprise was too good and tasty to sit on the table for long. Ali hugged Rishi and told him he would never forget this.

'It's almost like having your Abbu here for a few hours, on a visitor's visa,' Shehzad told his Pakistani housemate in a lighter vein, trying to lift the mood in the house.

The trio sat in the hall all of that night, listening to Ali talk about Abbu, Haji Sahib, Ammi and Lahori shaan. Before they slept, Shehzad etched a small bowl of curry on the wrists of all three. Curry was what had united them. A tattoo of love curry marked on them forever.

13

Zeenat returned home to a table laid out for dinner. Not feeling hungry, she locked herself in her room and shut out the world. Mullah knocked on her door a while later, but she was not in the mood to answer and sent him off from behind the closed door. All she wanted to do was to sit by the window and count the stars tonight. Something told her doing that could help her sleep. And yes, Don Williams too. His music lulled her to accept almost anything . . . But I believe in love . . . I believe in music . . . I believe in magic . . . I believe in you . . .

A wild flower, she had blossomed in the tinsel world of dreams and drama spun by Mullah and Fiza for their one and only child. Death, denial and post-truth were words that were somewhat new to her. She was growing up now. But was one day—one night—enough to grow up?

I'll never be in love again

My poor ol' heart will never mend
Oh, I'll find someone to hold now and then
But I'll never be in love again . . .

Mullah went back to his wife in a daze. His baby was an adult today, eighteen years old, and she was already shutting him out. He felt lifeless. She was his oxygen, the one who kept his heart pumping.

Fiza gathered him in her ample warmth and rubbed his neck and shoulder to keep the circulation going, massaging his temples to relieve the tension. 'Let her be,' she told him. 'Kids are like this . . . they need space to grow.'

Mullah had been telling himself the same thing. Yet . . .

Meanwhile, lost in the lights in the sky, Zeenat was searching for that one star to talk to. Her heart was overfull, but the vast sky gave her little solace.

Ten houses away, the boys had so much to tell each other that the night seemed short. 'It's the same in India,' Rishi let out after hearing Ali's Lahore story—featuring joint families, inheritance issues, bossy parents and interfering relatives.

'Exactly!' agreed Shehzad. 'In fact, it's shocking how uncannily similar we are even today.'

'Yes, it's uncanny!' Ali agreed, nodding in a daze.

'If we were one country, no one would have the balls to touch us—no one!' Rishi was now galloping off on his own track. 'A superpower we would be.'

'Getting visas on arrival . . . here, there . . . and everywhere!' A hundred emotions flitted through the Pakistani's face as he said this. Staring into the blackness of the night, he declared in a louder voice, 'We then wouldn't have needed their damn work permits. There would be enough to do at home.'

Shehzad sat up excitedly.

Rishi now couldn't resist teasing his lazy housemate. 'Our Bangla boy is so powered by the idea . . . think what will happen if his idle bones start working for us too.'

'Yes,' said Ali. 'He alone would raise our GDP by two per cent.'

Brushing off his housemates' ribbing, Shehzad said, 'Just think, what a cricket team we would have.' The Bangladeshi's eyes were shining. 'Kohli, Misbah, Dhoni, Shakib Al Hasan, Afridi, Mortaza . . .'

'Stop!' Rishi gagged him with a cushion. Shehzad could get really high on cricket.

'Okay, okay! It's not just cricket. Think—your Kashmir would also disappear.'

Rishi stared at him, unblinking. Had the tattoo boy finally lost it?

'I mean, your fight over Kashmir would disappear,' the Bangladeshi clarified.

'Yes,' Ali murmured, liking the idea. 'Our defence budget would get halved. And our military strength . . . it would triple.'

'The whole of Indian Ocean would be ours,' Rishi added, feeling powerful already. 'Our joint navy patrolling the waters, making the dragon go green.'

'China!' Shehzad tittered. 'The Asian top dog will forget to bark.'

Rishi agreed. 'The West will fear us and not Beijing then.'

With stars in their eyes and warmth in their hearts, the boys kept talking, thinking and dreaming big. It saved Ali from dealing with the gnawing emptiness within.

'The world will queue up to do business with us!' Rishi was zooming into heady times.

'We'll set up a new spice route,' the Pakistani chef proposed. 'Running through the whole of Central and West Asia, envied by every country in the world.'

The Dhaka boy clapped and cried out, 'Brilliant!'

'Think,' continued Rishi, winking at Ali as he spoke, 'about the ISI and RAW getting together! Then we'll get too wily for the world.'

The Pakistani could not stop himself then. He laughed heartily. A star shone brighter in the sky, saluting the friendly warmth on foreign soil that was lighting up a grieving heart.

'And that Security Council seat you've been begging for,' Shehzad said to Rishi, 'they'll offer it on a platter!'

'*Sahi farmaya*, janaab,' Ali patted Shehzad on the head. 'When hard-nosed netas from New Delhi and our suave diplomats team up, they'll bully the world to clinch us the best deals.'

'Your Taslima can ratchet up the volume for this,' Rishi pointed out to his Bangladeshi mate.

Yes, thought Shehzad. An activist who had not cowed down to bans or fatwas in Bangladesh or West Bengal; such a voice when it spoke for coming together of nations, it would mean a lot. The mention of Taslima Nasreen took Shehzad to Tagore and Kazi Nazrul Islam. 'It's not just about power. When our skies are one, even art and literature can bloom, wild and abundant.' His eyes became dreamy as he spoke. 'Bangla will work in concert with Urdu, not because it has to but because it wants to. Our new literature has much to gain from Urdu heritage. And Tagore—he has so much to tell everyone. Just like Nazrul.'

Rishi and Ali stared at their tattooed housemate, struck by his depth and vision. Shehzad had this way of surprising the hell out of them sometimes. He was generally so laid-back that when he chose to shine, he made them go flat, puncturing their egos totally.

Talk of art led to Bollywood, making Ali wistful. He was addicted to the latkas and jhatkas and over-the-top dialogues so typical of Bollywood. 'We'll get Karan Johar to shoot movies in Karachi with Bangladeshi heroines.'

'Our Bappa Mazumder can sing for SRK!' That was Shehzad.

'And your writers can pen some *real* content for our TV channels,' Rishi proposed, warming up to Ali's idea.

Was this even possible? Could their countries come together like they themselves had, and overturn history? There was so much baggage, so many wounds and niggles. Could they overcome it all in one day? Would their governments let them? The three sat thinking, going quiet all of a sudden.

What made it so impossible? Their hearts were in the right place. And yes, they did have a shared identity. In fact, a Pakistani from Lahore felt more in common with an Indian from Punjab than he did with a Muslim from Iraq. No doubt there were many hate-mongering people for whom it is a business to divide people. Unfortunately, they are the ones who walk the corridors of power or preach from religious pulpits. But what about the masses? Did they actually subscribe to the hysteria whipped up by their leaders and the media and the religious brokers? Were they really so gullible that they would harbour permanent hatred? It was a loaded question, pressing all three to look deep. But the answer to it was right there, staring them in the face.

'Here, in London, what does your border mean to you?' Rishi threw that to both Ali and Shehzad.

'Nothing,' replied Shehzad, without another thought.

'Nothing,' repeated Ali after him.

'See, that's it!' The Indian had put in words what the two had a vague idea about. 'Here, away from our mandir–masjid dealers and a jingoistic media, we're okay. We've no issues—none that we don't have with any other country in the world.'

'In fact, we're more comfortable with each other than with the Brits,' acknowledged Ali.

'Exactly! All that hate is pushed down our throats because it suits some people.'

'Meaning . . . if we cancel out their noise . . .' Shehzad paused as he said this, 'we are one again.'

Rishi and Ali looked at him and then at each other. The Bangladeshi had voiced what they too had concluded in their heads. They not only felt the same way, but they even thought the same way.

'Ai, dost, hamne tark-e-mohabbat ke bavzood, mehsoos ki hai teri zaroorat kabhi kabhi,' Ali signed off with Nasir Kazmi's poetry which had been echoing in his head again and again that night.

With the hope of a new tomorrow in their hearts, the three finally dropped off to sleep, casting off the shadow of death that had marred their day. That night, in house number 104, George Street, the borders of the subcontinent had truly melted.

14

More than the changed work profile or team dynamics, Rishi was taking time to adjust to the size of his new workplace. From the expanse of a car dealer's showroom and garage, he'd moved to a single-room unit cluttered with people, paper and computer terminals. Things were not so easy on the eye—or foot for that matter.

It was a tiny office with not many workers and the editor monitored most departments, including that of the new recruit. Not much happened at his desk, so Rishi was usually free to help others at their desks. He soon won many hearts and laurels—not for his stated skills or advertorial output, but for his steady and free-flowing advice. He doled out his pearls of wisdom to everyone—from the office boy to the illustrator to the editor. And his words worked—got them unruffled and raring to go again. Rishi had this inbuilt software that could analyse every change of mood accurately and help him to deal with it accordingly. His instant and out-of-the-box solutions were simple to apply and clicked for most people. The best part was he never squealed on anyone or judged them.

Even the editor had benefitted from his counselling. No wonder she was finding it tough to fire him despite his not bringing in the ads he had been employed to get. But Rishi did try his bit to increase the revenue for the paper. He dialled almost every baba and mata in town, seeking appointment, on some pretext or the other. And managed to connect with around a dozen of them but came back empty-handed.

The first one he met was a god-woman called Ma Anandamrignayani. Rishi spun tall stories to her, blathering on about how their desi readers were thirsty for divine guidance and were only waiting to be pointed to the right guru to achieve liberation. The mataji was almost hoodwinked into believing this sincere-sounding advertising executive. She was about to motion to one of her robed cronies to give him a cheque for a full-page ad when he did the unthinkable—he counselled her. Offering sage advice to a soul which was already supposed to be supremely enlightened was the ultimate blasphemy. Ma Anandamrignayani trembled with rage and cursed him for wasting her time. The cheque was clearly out of the question now. Instead, she asked him to check out of her ashram immediately!

Versions of this story were repeated in his encounters with other babas and matas. The end result was a long list of travel expenses with no sold ad space to show for it. The editor would've pulled her hair out in frustration had she not been sporting a cropped cut that could not be pulled at. Rishi stood in front of her, his head bowed, feeling suitably ashamed and helpless. He kept trying to sooth her frayed nerves.

She was about to fire him, and feeling awfully guilty about it, but she had a timely brainwave.

'Rishi, you can't stay in the ad department, you know . . .' she began.

He made it easier for her by nodding in complete understanding without meeting her eye.

'However . . .'

He looked up now. 'However' was a powerful word, carrying limitless possibilities.

'You could do the thing you're good at. Start a new column for the paper. On relationships.'

Rishi went numb. Relationships? He'd been unable to keep his own, and she wanted him to sustain a column? Life was such a sick joke!

'A simple, heart-to-heart question–answer piece it will be, counselling desi girls and boys. You'll be their agony aunt. No, uncle.'

He struggled to find his voice, clearing his throat multiple times. 'But . . . ma'am . . . I've never done this . . . not this way . . . never wrote it out . . . I . . . I don't think I could do it.'

Her eyes had gone hard and glacial now. His hesitation was his problem, because she couldn't give him any more leeway. 'Well . . . it's up to you. It's this . . . or nothing.'

Rishi took not a second to say yes then. He wasn't ready to win the Asian title for being booted out a record number of times. The ad sales executive had a sudden makeover that morning—as an agony uncle. And he slipped into his new role as if he had been doing it all his life. He became an instant hit. The column was welcomed with a mountain of mails. The island seemed cluttered with confused and heartbroken desis. Hundreds of letters and emails arrived from all over London, seeking advice, comfort and clarity on relationship complexities. His was thankfully a desk job with no public interface. There was not even a byline announcing his name. Only an email address for correspondence. Such complete anonymity worked perfectly for Rishi.

The agony uncle soon became the lifeline for every silly, serious and outrageous problem that plagued local subcontinental hearts; he solved them without fuss, deploying his patient voice and palatable formulae. From dating sob stories to mother-in-law antics, fantasy date analysis to the consequences of marrying a rich and cultured girl pockmarked with pimples—Rishi dealt with them all.

A woman complained that while her father-in-law jumped to compliment her, the husband rarely noticed what she was wearing. 'Return the favour to your father-in-law with added honey,' he advised, 'and make sure your husband and mother-in-law watch and hear you do it.'

A man wanted to know if he should marry his girlfriend simply because she was handy and his parents were insistent. 'Not just handy, she should be someone you can handle for long,' he told him. As for parental pressure, he warned it was an Asian malaise that required immediate vaccination.

Reassuring but forthright, his wry humour and non-judgemental tone made him wildly popular. He connected with his audience well and soon became a voice that the readers trusted. What he couldn't do as an advertising sales executive, he managed now as a columnist—contributing hugely to the revenue of the paper by increasing readership manifold. The heart of *Desi Beats* now beat with him. A laptop and the cheapest brand of whiskey available were his constant companions in his march to glory.

The British desis were smitten by this new agony uncle, but much to their agony, no one knew who he was. Even his housemates knew Rishi only as a copy editor. Guarding his new identity zealously, he went about his business quietly as usual.

15

Shehzad got up early despite not sleeping most of the night. It was only six o'clock. This was very unlike him, for he was a heavy eater and a sound sleeper. Not bothering to take a shower, he downed a black coffee and took off, not telling anyone where he was headed.

Ali saw him leave, and Rishi only heard him. Before the Pakistani could digest that it was actually the Bangladeshi that he was seeing up and awake at this hour, he had already left. The Indian assumed it was Ali messing around with his pots and pans, creating a racket at this godforsaken hour. The thought of Shehzad being up and about at this time of the day was something even his sleep-befuddled mind couldn't conceive.

Shehzad walked purposefully down George Street to the Tube station. He took the Metropolitan Line, overruling every instinct that begged him not to continue through to

King's Cross, St Pancras, Euston Square, Great Portland Street, Baker Street, Finchley Road, Wembley Park, Preston Road, Northwick Park and finally to Harrow on the Hill. Arriving at the station, he staggered out like a zombie, and walked and walked till he reached where he'd set out for— South Harrow Lane.

Then he stopped. Despite coming this far, he was finding it impossible to move an inch further. His feet suddenly felt like lead and his palms went cold. It became a struggle to pull up his foot—glued as it was to the pavement—and take a step forward. Actually, it was going backwards—going back to a time and zone that he loathed. And yet, here he was. He pushed himself to go past every house till he reached number 121. Then he froze.

The white gate of the brown-and-orange house was a border he simply could not cross. Not that anyone had stopped him there—no one but himself. He just stood there. Looking. Staring at the door. The windows. The spacious garden. So much stuff was hurtling down his mental plane, some blurred, some sharp and piercing. Like a roller coaster, it looped him high, then dropped him steep, plunging him through fuzzy spirals that terrified him. One thing collided with another, making him go crazy. His stomach churned. Shehzad wanted to scream but had lost his voice.

Why had he come here? He had jumped off the deep end unthinkingly. Life was a wicked twister, he should've known better. Why confront something he would never be ready for? It was madness, sheer madness to come here. Minutes passed. An hour. Hours. He stood there like a statue, cracked up. Fighting himself on the inside, and impassive and unmoving on the outside. But how long could he stand there? He had to get himself together, pick up the pieces and walk on—or sink. So he took a deep breath, made a decision and moved forward. Crossing the garden, Shehzad walked bravely up to the front porch, right up to the door. Found a bell there. It was time, he told himself, and reached out to ring it.

But something blasted inside him, throwing him back, and charring every piece of him till there was nothing left—nothing but tears. Tears that washed away his bravado, his air of invincibility. Carrying him away . . . far, far away from this house, this street, its people . . . and their power to destroy.

Shehzad did not directly take the Tube back home. He rode the Tube in one direction and then another, wanting to lose himself. It was sunset when he found himself back on George Street.

Rishi saw him walk in. This was a different guy. A broken man. Shorn of the swagger Shehzad was famous for. The Indian took a minute to swallow this. There were twenty things he wanted to ask, but held himself back. Clearly, Shehzad was not in a state to answer questions.

Shehzad did not see Rishi, or the sofa or the table or even the fridge, which was always his first stop every time he entered the house. All he registered now was the door to his room. A door that he staggered through and banged hard behind him to shut out the world.

Rishi gave him an hour before he knocked. Sixty minutes, in his estimation, were enough to seethe, mope or allow things to sink in. If you needed more time, you actually needed help. Or, at least, that's how he saw it. And he knocked again. Getting no answer, he marched in, uninvited. His pupils dilated to make sense of the dark room. He discerned an outline by the bed. That was his friend. At once, he was by his side, just sitting there. Saying nothing. Sometimes, you only need someone to sit next to you. You don't want them to say anything. A silent presence could be hugely comforting and Rishi understood this.

In the dark, two heads flung back against the bed, tried to figure things out, not knowing if they were worth figuring out. The evening dimmed to night, but it mattered not in this room. It was dark before and so it remained.

Thirsty, Rishi got up. Shehzad, surprisingly, was neither thirsty nor hungry. He hadn't invited Rishi to come in. He didn't stop him from going. Only one thing he registered—his room was his alone once again.

Hydrated, Rishi could think more clearly. He had known for quite some time that there was something eating Shehzad. Had seen it peep past the Bangla swagger. What he saw today was the shell his housemate had become. This scared him; he feared for his friend. If the broken frame did not vent out what was destroying him, it would be a funeral of all hope.

There was no choice. Rishi the counsellor had to intervene. He had to find the right weapon to slay the monsters and set his friend free. Armed with the infinite patience and wisdom that experience forces on to you, the Indian marched back into the dark to rescue his favourite Bangladeshi.

Shehzad had shifted from the floor to his desk. Oblivious to the help being launched from across the border, he waged his battle with his own weapons.

Rishi found the tattoo artist sketching. Furious black lines coalesced into what looked like two eyes, a nose, hoop earrings . . . and the rest was a blur. Looked abstract, but was a face for sure . . . a woman's face.

It's always a woman, cursed Rishi.

He slashed it then. Knifed his sketch. Cutting the face first with a thick, angry line and then with a paper knife. Shehzad smiled as he slashed it into two. It was a smile that hurt. Watching him in silence, Rishi felt his pain. It was too acute to be counselled. Walking up to Shehzad's desk, Rishi bent to pick up the fallen half of the torn sketch. The lines were smudged with tears.

Rishi returned it to the artist with a compliment and a question: 'Why a paper knife when you got more muscle than me?'

16

Spicy, tender and juicy—just like his tarkewali curried beef nihari. Well, if she was the nihari, he wanted to be her khameeri roti, the perfect match for such a delectable dish.

Ali was smitten. Zeenat did this to him. He had been having delicious, aromatic dreams about her ever since he'd first laid eyes on her. A glorious mix of a dozen strong and spicy scents assailed him every time she came near, stoking both his hunger and heartbeat. So appetizing to look at, piping hot in her ways, and sweeter and more fragrant than his pista kheer, Zeenat made him want to be utterly gluttonous.

To call her a tempting dish would be a severe insult. She was a heavenly creation—a gorgeous mix of seasoning, texture, scent and flavour. Never had any girl enticed him so. He liked talking to her, he enjoyed hearing her talk. Her madness. Her sweetness. When she acted sour. When she became naughty. Everything about her whet his appetite like nothing else did.

Was he in love? Ali lay in bed, thinking. Wondering. Well, no one made him feel as much on fire as she did. He felt shy and tender around her, and talkative too. She stirred conflicting feelings in him, melting him with just a look, a word . . . a touch. This must surely be love.

Ali began to pace his bedroom, and then took to the living room, mumbling,

Yeh mujhe chain kyon nahin parta?
Ek hi shakhs tha jahaan mein kya?

Only Jaun Elia seemed to understand his condition. What about Zeenat? How did she see him? Did she feel the same? Did she find him as irresistible? Or was he just a regular dish—no big deal?

Khub hain shauk ka yeh pehlu bhi
Main bhi barbaad ho gaya, tu bhi.

Ali was full of love and doubt and anxiety. With girls, you never can tell. But how could he know for sure? 'Approach her,' cajoled a voice from inside. Yes, that was the only way. He would make a subtle approach. Girls liked that.

But then he was not Shehzad. That Dhaka fellow always gabbed with her to the skies and back. Not a shy bone in his body had he! Why couldn't he be like Shehzad? Uninhibited, saying and doing whatever struck him. He was that way with some but . . . but not with her. Why? He didn't know for sure. Perhaps love made you that way. Shehzad clearly had no such hurdle.

Ali decided he would go to her, snatch some moments together. Outside. Just the two of them. His love-struck heart jumped from one thought to another. Should he take her something? Girls liked gifts. But what could he give her? It had to be something special. Flowers . . . chocolate . . . perfume . . .

No. That was not him at all. He would not copy those around him. Ali would give her something totally his own, a slice of his heart. It struck him then. The perfect gift—shahi tukda! Yes, that Mughal sweet was fit for her majesty. He would make it for her right then, with saffron and cardamom and . . . The chef spent the next half hour in the kitchen, whipping up a treat for his love.

Soon after, laden with sweetness, he rang the bell at Zeenat's house. Thankfully, it was she who answered. Surprised to see Ali at her door, she wanted to ask what he was doing there but stopped herself. Ali had brought her shahi tukda. That was sweet of him, but she was not fond of sweets. They messed up her system totally. She opened her mouth to tell him that, but couldn't. It was good to see him get over his grief and start living again. No, she couldn't prick his happy bubble. Inviting him in, she put the shahi tukda in the fridge and offered him a drink.

'Not today,' he said, and then apologized profusely for refusing.

It didn't matter to Zeenat if he drank or not, so she changed the subject. She checked on his family in Lahore and learnt that they were coping. She didn't know what else to say.

Ali gushed when she asked about them. She was interested in his family! Surely, that meant she was interested in him. His pain was her pain.

Zeenat waited for him to continue. Ali sat with a stupid smile plastered on his face, saying nothing. She was okay with this too. She was comfortable with silence in his company. Actually, it felt good to have him around. He didn't mess up her head in any way. Not like . . .

Ali saw her mind wander off; no, that would not do. He wanted her back, engrossed only in his own world, so he proposed a walk. A short walk.

Zeenat knew not how to respond to this.

'We'll carry our headphones,' he said, wanting to quell any objections. 'You listen to your music. I'll listen to mine. We'll get some fresh air. Exercise!' And he successfully sold the idea to her. Together they left, headphones plugged in, in step with each other but musically apart. She with her Zayn Malik. He with his Sahir Ludhianvi.

'Maybe it's the way she walked . . . through the doors and past the guards'. Zayn made her swoon. 'And we danced all night to the best song ever, we knew every line . . .'

Tuned finely to her moods, 'vas happening', Zayne's music seemed to ask, questioning the new vibes coursing through her. Reminding her of Shehzad . . . of her birthday night and their dance . . . pepping her up instantly.

He swayed to the lilt of the ghazal.

Pyar par bas to nahin hai mera, lekin phir bhi
Tu bata de tujhse pyar karu ya na karu . . .

Thandi hawa aein, lehrake ayein, rut hain jawaan, tum ho
yahan . . .

The words were soft and haunting, letting out what his heart was singing silently.

They walked on, each in their own space. Not speaking. Listening. But not to each other.

Ali stole a glance at her ever so often, and he found her looking straight ahead each time. There was so much he wanted to say, and much more that he wanted to ask. But he did neither. Instead, he offered her his music and asked for hers in return.

Zeenat was too zapped by his request to refuse. Wordless, she handed over her headphones and took his.

Man re tu kahe na dheer dhare
Woh nirmohi moh na jaane . . .

She struggled with the words 'nirmohi moh' and checked with Ali what they could possibly mean.

'Silent fascination,' he told her.

Made no sense to her—the beat, the words—it all went over her head. She listened, but with half an ear.

Ali plugged into her music enthusiastically.

Shot me out of the sky
You're my kryptonite
You keep making me weak
Yeah, frozen and can't breathe . . .

And got zoned out. What was this kryptonite? He turned to Zeenat. She was hearing Ludhianvi Sahib. He did not want to disturb. 'Cause you've got that one thing . . .' This was not his kind of music. Yet, he tried hard to like it. Wasn't that what you're supposed to do when in love? Adapt? He wasn't sure but gave it a shot.

Zeenat was done. The walk . . . the ghazal . . . the clutter in her head. All of it beat her down till she went crazy.

'Ali?'

'Shall we turn back?' he asked, understanding at once.

He'd had a wonderful hour and a half with her and was now all charged up to sweat it out in life at the Nawab Balti tonight.

Zeenat was thankful he did not ask for more. She did not have the heart to give in or refuse, for that matter.

17

The nose had been sliced through diagonally. One hoop earring fluttered in his left hand, a hint of a cheek and some hair showing. The remainder was on the floor. *As is my life*, thought Shehzad. Torn and tattered. Existing in bits. Till Rishi picked up the pieces and handed them to him, asking him to make them whole again.

Rishi? What was he doing in the room? Invading his sacred space. Twice in one day. Didn't he know better? Shehzad turned to blast the Indian for gatecrashing. Wanted to dump all his anger on the . . . He never got a chance. The idiot gathered him in a hug, startling him and draining him of his ability to think or curse. The Bangladeshi froze. He was not used to such show of emotion, it made him uncomfortable. No one had reached out to him this way, as far as he could remember.

Baba? Baba was a long-forgotten statistic in the family calculations. Ma was the most visible presence in their household even after she'd left the house—*especially* after she'd left.

Letting go of Shehzad, Rishi blinked. What had come over him? He'd never been the hugging sort. He looked at Shehzad, unsure of what to do. The fellow looked hollow, no colour, no dude act. In fact, he looked dark. It must be the room, Rishi thought, in shadows as it was. Why this boy did not switch on lights was beyond him. But something about Shehzad was still not right. He was breathing and yet not breathing. *That's it!* That's what made him embrace the guy, shocking the hell out of both of them.

Once the hug was done, Rishi was at ease. His housemate looked uneasy though. There was that sketch too, the sliced halves hanging before them, as mysterious as the Bermuda Triangle and equally unsafe. Rishi knew not what he risked if he dared to question the hyper fellow about the knifed sketch.

The hug had transported Shehzad into another world, one where there were no hugs, no kisses, no warmth. Only cold abandonment. People didn't gather you there. They left you for good, unconcerned about what befell you afterwards.

He heard the door bang shut as she walked out with her bags. Bang! Harder. Louder. Till he could take it no more and fell on the chair, sealing his ears with both hands. The door had banged shut only once, that too, many years ago, but he kept hearing it again and again. The noise getting more deafening with each passing year.

Startled, Rishi rushed to him, dropping down next to his chair. He did not know this Shehzad and was not sure how to deal with him. But pain—he knew pain. He recognized it all too well, and had learnt to handle it like a pro. So he waited for it to all pour out. Not asking. Not hurrying. Giving it time to spill out.

'Bitch! Bitch!'

Shehzad was angry—and in tears, only he didn't let them flow. With a hand that shook, he grabbed the shredded sketch, balled up the pieces and flung them across the room.

Rishi saw it land in a far corner. 'Shehzad . . .'

That did it. He burst out like he hadn't for years, hitting the desk with his fist, throwing back his head and crying like hell. His face contorted, his body trembling. 'How could she? How could she?'

Rishi gripped Shehzad's hand lest he hurt himself.

'They're all the same . . .' Rishi couldn't stop himself. He spoke from experience.

'Same?' Shehzad was furious then. 'Your mom's the same, huh?' He gripped Rishi's collar and stared at him, his eyes crazed. 'Your ma ran off with her husband's friend, did she?'

Rishi's heart sank. This was too black, way out of his depth.

'Took off like just like that! *Snap!* You sit watching, not crying, just watching . . . watch Ma go . . . watch Baba go too—to the dogs!'

Shehzad got up with a start. Even the chair was beginning to hurt. All because of that damn Pakistani! She left them for him. Chose him and a life in London with him; she found her life in Dhaka no longer bright. Londoni is what she wanted to be. So she dumped them. Like yesterday's trash. He slammed his fist against the wall. Hurting it. But feeling nothing. It was so bad inside, his fist felt just fine. He had not understood why she left when she banged the door shut. The truth bomb hit him much later, when the neighbours began to sing, retelling her story in vivid detail, gossiping about how she was queening it up in London while her family rotted back home.

He had tracked her down then—right up to her house in South Harrow Lane. The one he took the Tube to this morning. He zoomed in on her address the day he landed at Heathrow. That was why he had come to London—to find her. He knew not what he'd do when he found her. But find her he must. It took him months to muster up the guts to go up that road. He would go near and come back each time. Today, he made it to her door. But that insecure monster inside him pulled him back. What if she didn't want him still . . . and rejected him outright? What if he lost control and did something he'd regret?

Rishi felt Shehzad's load weigh him down too. So he kept sitting on the floor, while Shehzad vented it out. On the walls, going from one corner to another, till his battery drained out and he flopped on to the bed.

'How old were you?' Rishi asked.

Shehzad took five minutes to reply. 'Not even six.'

God!

'I saw her today,' Shehzad confessed in a whimper. 'Her house actually.'

So that's where he had been coming from this noon, looking ghastly and chalky. *No wonder!* The pieces were now fitting in Rishi's puzzled head. The Agra lad dragged himself up on to Shehzad's chair and stared at his friend sprawled on the sheets, eyes tightly shut, but awake. His past was screwing his present, etching itself on him like the tattoos he etched on human skin.

The blank sketch pad on the desk teased him, reminding Rishi of the slashed face that haunted this room. She seemed to be everywhere—in his room, his mind, and his bloody world. He had to rid Shehzad of her. Now. But how? How do you purge yourself of a face? How? Yes, so simple it was—with another face. 'Shehzad,' he said, walking up to his friend and throwing the pad at him.

The Bangladeshi's eyes flew open at this new weight on his chest. His pad.

'Shehzad, see if you can sketch another.'

What the hell was this fellow saying? Had he lost it? Shehzad was not in a state to focus on Rishi or his gibberish.

Rishi shook him then and thrust the pad into his hands. 'Sketch one more face, bro. But this time, make it a happy face.'

Shehzad examined the Agra specimen, his eyes dilating in wonder. This one was definitely not from the same planet as him. No way!

'A face,' continued Rishi, 'that makes you happy. And fills you with love. Sketch that face.'

Leaving the Bangladeshi artist to take on this challenge, Rishi walked out the door, hoping the demons of yesterday would walk out with him.

18

The agony uncle was hard at work. His inbox was overflowing with every Bangla, Lankan, Hindustani and Pakistani lonely heart clamouring for his attention. And advice. One wanted to know how to rid herself of her selfie-obsessed boyfriend. Another desired a Buddhist partner willing to chant with her. One guy was keen to spread world peace but complained his wife wasn't cooperating. Added to this were dozens of queries from late bloomers on how to date confidently. Several ugly ducklings wanted him to suggest a magic makeover that could snag them handsome princes. Some wanted to know if guys who were not obsessed with beauty actually existed. All of them expected the moon from their agony uncle and believed he could supply the same.

He sure tried, giving a bit of his head and heart to each reader who wrote to him. Spreading his life knowledge evenly across every query that popped his way. But there was this one reader who was forcing him to dig deep within for buried truths, and then playing hockey with his mind and emotions. She was slowly and surely worming her way into his soul. Her sadness first drilled a hole into his heart. Her questions pushed him to scratch beneath the surface of his emotions, stretching his mind and psyching him up to change his own goalposts even as he anticipated her next shot. It was a complicated formation, and Rishi did his best to comfort her, but she deflected every move he made, fouling his advances with a stick with which she beat herself.

'Adopted'. For her, that was a dirty word. No matter how hard he tried to launder it, she still saw it as an indelible stain, marring her life. To find out that your mother is not your mother, and your father not really your father can be terrifying. It had destroyed her completely, turning her morose and miserable. That's when she found him, had burrowed into him, wanting to know which soil she should call her own now. For, the earth that this earthworm knew was no longer hers.

Rishi was stricken. Her raw wound's hurt bled on to him. Her emails, dripping red, affecting him like he thought he would never be affected again. She called him her own because she knew nothing and no one that she truly owned now. That was so like him, he thought. He too spread himself everywhere as he had not a slice that was his very own.

Identifying with her loss of identity, he plunged deeper into her mails and found insecurities festering everywhere. He tried to slough them away, giving her space to breathe. But it wasn't that easy. While understanding her dilemmas, her fears and her uncertainty, he was confronted by his own monsters. Doubts and insecurities lurking within him raised their anxious heads, taunting him, questioning his role. What he could not do for himself, how could he do for anyone else? That was logical, but sometimes he reasoned, while helping others, you can actually help yourself.

He began by offering her a foothold in life. Her mails revealed she was on the edge and that scared him. What if she felt so alone that she wanted to give up? No. He had to stop her. To do that, first he had to get her to trust him, and he did that by hearing her out. She told him about her dad who had not just been the pillar but also the walls and roof of her life. He had cocooned her with so much affection that she did not know how to think, smile or dance now that this sheath was gone. Rishi tried to explain that the sheath still existed if she wanted it to. But she was too taken up with the DNA angle to listen to him.

Her heart heavier than stone, she confided in him all that burdened her.

When he kissed my knee when I fell, it was not my dad who had kissed me. The stories of my great-grandfather that he told me at bedtime were not a part of my legacy. They took care of my aches as a child only to give me such heartache when I grew up. It can never be the same again. Everything is unravelling.

The worst part was she had no idea who her biological parents were. No clue to reveal where she came from and this upset Rishi too. What if this were to happen to him? How would he react? Would he respond adequately? Could he keep his head sane when nothing else was? Families were toppling like houses of cards everywhere. Ali had lost his Abbu. Shehzad had an Ammi who had abandoned him. And now this girl. Life could really be such a shithole.

Well, if no one else, Rishi decided he would be there for her. He would keep writing to her and help her get past her shock, no matter how long it took. He would hold her hand when she was low, and cheer her on every step of the way.

The agony uncle was agonizing far too much over one reader and this became a problem too. So he consulted an agony aunt in another publication, asking how to save an agony aunt from drowning in a reader's issues. His mail was ignored. That got his goat, but opened his eyes to the fact that readers in his own paper would be smarting the same way when their letters were ignored.

So he unwrapped himself from his singular reader's misery and got busy advising everyone again, addressing every father-in-law to high-school girl who approached him for any grouse under the sun. Till a new and bigger problem sprouted in his own backyard, forcing the uncle to drop his avuncular role for once.

19

Allah be praised, the Indian had finally left. Shehzad had the room, his space and its darkness all to himself again. That's what he was used to. Sharing, caring hugs and sympathy were taboo in his galaxy. How dare Rishi rewrite his rules! Any future invasion would be aggressively dealt with. Yes, he would guard his solitariness till the last millisecond.

Even as he mentally framed a list of suitable punishments befitting the crime of trespassing, along with a string of choicest swear words to ward off unwanted sympathizers, his mind kept drifting to what Rishi had said. *Sketch another face. A happy one. One that makes you happy.*

He cursed. So sharp and insightful was this fellow, it was as if he had two heads. Thankfully, he rarely employed them both at once. Why today then? Spewing so much wisdom when none was sought? Also, Rishi's repeat infiltration of his space this evening definitely smelt of a misplaced feeling of entitlement. He probably thought he was getting even for all the Bangladeshis walking across the Indian border all these years. Well, he wasn't dumb to allow this like the Indian government did. Barging into his room and life without permission was fraught with deadly consequences.

The atmosphere in the room had changed subtly, without the occupant being aware of it. The light was now on and South Harrow Lane had been forgotten. It looked like Rishi had invaded not just the physical space but skilfully stomped into his housemate's mental domain too. Diverting Shehzad's mind from the past to focus on the pest inhabiting his present. This mental invasion brought its own collateral benefit— Shehzad forgot the tears and fears clogging his happiness, and breathed freely and deeply. His battery too had surprisingly got charged enough to make him fidgety. Thinking up dire penalties for Rishi had also upped his mood considerably, so he quit the bed and moved to his desk.

'Get back to work!' he told himself. The studio catalogue was crying for newer designs. He needed to check on scheduled appointments and order the carbon tattoo needles he had been putting off buying. Warming his ass on the bed or chair wouldn't help because there was too much work, so he got slaving. Scrolling down his appointments for the next day, he was distracted by a white triangle jutting out from under one corner of his laptop. It turned out to be his sketch pad. Pulling it out, he propped it on his laptop and stared at it, his appointments forgotten.

The blank sheet beckoned him, calling him to create something. He kept looking at the pad, considering something, then finally picked up his Staedtler Fineliner pen and began to draw thick bold lines. His hand flew across the paper, for it knew what was in his head and heart. Within minutes, he had an outline. Shehzad began shading it, darkening the strokes to highlight every prominent feature, smudging at places. Next, detailing the sketch with light and heavy shading till he captured the depth and perfection he wanted.

Satisfied, he put down his pen and picked up the sketch to examine his artwork. It had a nice feeling to it. He felt its energy and sparkle, right from the bounce in the hair to the merriment in the eyes, not forgetting the dramatic expression that looked so fake, and yet so cute. It made him smile. But the next second, he froze. It was Zeenat! He had sketched her face! He had not meant to. It just happened. Even while he was drawing, he had been unaware of the face he was capturing.

'Sketch a face . . . one that makes you happy,' Rishi's challenge echoed in the room.

Was it Rishi invading his head now? That bloody idiot! He couldn't influence a rat—no way could he dare mess with Shehzad's mind. No, this was surely his own insanity. He was going mad. *Mad about her.* Shehzad jumped at this voice, and looked around him—there was no one. The voice had floated up from inside him, catching him by the throat, expelling every ounce of oxygen existing in his lungs and leaving him gasping.

This was new territory. Shehzad had never felt this deeply about any girl. He was unfeeling—or so he'd told himself and the world. Then how had she marched into his heart? With an unsteady hand, he picked up the sketch again and ran his fingers over her hair, the black locks flying all over the place even in his drawing. He examined her nose, sharp and pert; her almond eyes, huge, expressive and flooded with Bollywood dreams.

He caressed the sketch, tracing her angular face, seeing her with new eyes. Zeenat! When did this happen? When had he got so caught in her, without even realizing it? What a jerk he was! Blind to the madness brewing inside him. 'Zeenie!' he cried out. 'You got me, baby. Damn you!'

Feeling light-headed, he marched up and down the room, talking to himself, smiling stupidly, then frowning, and then smiling again. 'You knew?' he asked the dragons, birds and butterflies pinned on his walls. 'You saw us here, every time . . . surely you knew . . .? And you!' He pinched the poster girl and asked, 'Why didn't you warn me?'

Punching his world for hiding this truth from him, Shehzad fell on the bed, high and euphoric. Strangely, he didn't feel hungry tonight. Did love kill your appetite? If he'd known, he would've swum the Channel to escape her. Another hour went by. Shehzad spent it with himself, relishing the taste of this new feeling, desiring no company. Not even chicken tonight.

It was past midnight when it struck him that he still hadn't eaten. What the bloody hell! She had taken his heart, that too without asking, and that was okay. But his appetite? Love wasn't supposed to wreck stomachs. Hell, no!

20

Fiza and Mullah were on exactly the same wavelength today. Her London-born-and-bred culture and thinking was, for a change, not clashing with her imported-from-India-and-made-British husband. Both were overwhelmingly in favour of seeing Zeenat engaged as soon as possible. Though Fiza felt superior to her husband in every way, she knew he had far more leverage with their one and only daughter and so she asked him to approach her.

The entire course of action had already been charted out meticulously inside her head; one by one, she would reveal her cards. Fiza was not just looking to get her girl married off and settled, she also had the right boy in mind. Someone hailing from a similar background, ethnicity, religion, devoutness and even skin colour. Not having much of an extended family here in England from which to pluck a potential son-in-law, her choices had been limited. Yet, she had stumbled upon a prize catch. Call it her baby's kismet.

Her husband had switched sides, leaving his daughter, to side with the mother for this one battle. A diehard romantic in his salad days, Mullah had ripened into a practical and worldly person who wanted all the comfort and stability of an arranged marriage for his princess. Fiza wanted to sneak in her proposal through another party. She wanted to throw a bash that included the prospective groom and served to brighten his prospects. Mullah preferred a direct attack, and for once, he won.

At the dinner table, before everyone got busy with the salad and kebabs, Mullah came straight to the point. 'Zeenat, your Ammi and I think . . . it's time you got engaged.' Pausing for a few seconds, he continued, 'We'll find you a good boy . . . someone who's honest, down-to-earth and not shy of commitment. Someone from our own community, someone who'll keep you as happy as we do.'

That was it, Mullah exhaled in relief, having managed to pull off a nice, clean surgical strike—timing it right and dwelling on all the important points. Before he could pat himself again for offloading this delicate and difficult topic, his limited strike had inflated into a full-blown war.

Zeenat raged and ranted, losing it completely like she'd seen Bollywood heroes do on screen whenever there was a major travesty. 'Marry . . . Marry me off? Just who . . . who gave you this right?' Banging down her fork on the half-eaten kebab, she threw back her chair and strode up to her father. 'Am I your pet to keep, feed and then parcel off when you feel like it?' At full volume, she blasted him, firing point-blank to check their shameless encroachment into her personal life.

Unprepared for her extreme reaction, Mullah tried to reason that this was for the best. 'When did you get so feudal?' Zeenat questioned him sharply, looking at her mother as she spoke, knowing fully well where it was all coming from.

'Zeenat . . . we only want you to be happy . . . trust me.'

'You butt out of my life completely! And now!' She hit back, pushing out the one person who occupied her heart and life till now.

Mullah went white with shock. Fiza was suitably distraught, but she had known it would not be easy to persuade their obstinate girl. Inhaling deeply, she stepped into the fight to finish what Mullah had started. Reinforcing the general sentiment of families, which swung in favour of children getting engaged at the right age, Fiza droned on about how Zeenat needed a man who was patient, educated, from a decent family and who 'had an understanding of religion and values'.

'Does he need to have a beard too?' Zeenat cut in with a sneer. She was smarting at this dual attack. 'And tell me,' she said, bouncing up to her mother, 'What should be his ideal weight? Come on, tell me! How many pounds?'

Fiza brushed it off as a childish tantrum and tried diplomacy next. 'You've always been so special, Zeenat. We want you to have the best, and arrange the best for you—for all time.'

'You'll arrange for it, huh?' Zeenat was fast losing control. 'Arrange for marriage, arrange for love too, will you? And sex?' Her voice had gone deadly low and threatening. 'All home delivered, huh?'

Fiza refused to be provoked. Reaching out to her daughter, she explained in measured tones, 'When you have the respect and trust of a man, love will automatically develop.'

'Jeez!' Zeenat grew hysterical then. 'Automatically develop!' Repeating her mother's insane, illogical words in a sing-song voice, Zeenat kept prancing round and round the dining table as if part of some bizarre tableau being enacted there.

'Which planet do you come from?' she asked Fiza. 'I don't know you.'

Mullah sat through it all, suffering her act, not adding another word or gesture.

'You two . . . you . . . ' Picking up a fork, she pointed at the two people at the table who were trying to live her life for her, and said, 'Such experts you are! When to marry, who to marry, how to love . . . you know everything!'

Fiza did not get where all this was leading to. But Mullah was getting more jittery by the minute. He knew his dramatic daughter was reaching some climax.

'Take your shit to the world and charge them for it . . . you guys are so good at it! Arrange for spouses, families . . . fix them all up . . . do it for pounds . . . thousands of pounds. But leave me . . . leave me alone.'

All of this drama was now disturbing Fiza. She was quintessentially British and therefore, not used to such an excessive show of emotion. And pounds—what was this talk of pounds?

'Matchmake for the whole bloody community, I give a damn. Don't you dare with me!' Zeenat screamed, stopping her mom right there as she was about to dispense another of her prim and proper and artfully logical statements.

'Zeenat!' Mullah intervened. By taking only her name, he was trying to let her know she had crossed some borders, and that was unacceptable.

But you cannot roll up a drama queen when she is in full flow. Mullah knew this and looked on helpless. 'Go freak out there, headhunting brides and grooms . . . killing freedom . . . murdering love . . . go . . .'

One part of Mullah was enjoying her histrionics. *Such talent!* It was being wasted in this house and country. She was custom-made for Bollywood, his baby. His princess. But the husband and father in him disagreed with this rebellious thought and ordered him to remember his role and think and act accordingly. Fiza continued to bear the brunt of Zeenat's rage.

'You'll make thousands,' Zeenat spat. 'Sell them the full package—spouse background check, lifestyle compatibility check, match for age, height and weight, and any other stupid detail you can think of. Do it! Enjoy yourself at their expense.'

If it weren't so tragic, it would be funny, thought the head of the family.

Then Fiza made a classic statement. 'For this day, we brought you up?'

And something snapped inside Zeenat. She left them. Walked out without another word. Neither Mr nor Mrs Mullah had the guts to ask where she was going.

21

Her heart heavy and confused, Zeenat trundled along, not knowing where she should go. Just one thing she knew—no way could she go back home tonight. Ten houses up the street, she paused, her feet braking automatically. Technically, wasn't this house also hers? As for the tenants, they were no longer just tenants but an important and dependable chunk of her personal life. So staying the night here should be okay. In fact, it was a two-in-one deal. She would get here most of the comforts she got at home and still be able to sulk it out in the eyes of the older folk. Add to it the company of the boys. So she rang the doorbell, still angry but anticipating her mood to rapidly change for the better.

Her next hour went in recounting the horrors that befell her at house number 94. Her life was being auctioned off by Mullah and his *biwi*, she told them in between loud sniffles. It was a box office show featuring heavy dialogues, over-the-top emotions, frantic gestures, and tears that fell right on cue. Shehzad and Ali bent over backwards to console the stricken beauty, and in righteous anger, vowed to be her knights in shining armour, brave enough to take on even their own landlord, that too, in a foreign land.

Zeenat was impressed by this guarantee of support. She could now quit worrying over parental infringement of her personal space and proceed to have a good time with her friends. Yet, a tiny part of her was still miffed with the events of the evening and this came in the way of her enjoying full throttle.

Shehzad had the perfect answer to this. 'Try Ali's mutton curry. It's famous for its healing powers.'

'What?'

'Yes, Zeenie! It can warm your heart, mood and belly all at once.'

She knew not what to say. Their concern was bowling her over. Shehzad took her silence to mean she wasn't convinced, so kept selling the curry to her.

'Have a bowl and every stinker will get blown . . . into oblivion—I guarantee it!'

Ali just kept nodding. Zeenat was in tears. The smitten suitors rushed up to her with tissues, wanting to repair the damage they had caused unwittingly.

'Silly, I'm not crying because I'm sad—I'm happy! You guys have made me happy.' Their care and promise of curry had driven her to the edge again—a happy edge this time.

Reassured, the cook and his assistant took off for the kitchen. Rishi walked in just then and was promptly requisitioned for kitchen duty. Zeenat hovered around them and entertained the workers with her tales that defied logic but were within the realm of imagination.

That night she sat sandwiched between Ali and Shehzad, facing the Indian, gorging on curry that was refilled with aplomb even before she'd managed to finish half her bowl. Life sucked, but it did have its moments, she accepted grudgingly.

Their tummies full, they moved to the sofa and cushions in the living room, with Zeenat getting the seat of honour—the central seat on the three-seater sofa. Her two knights flanked her on each side just in case any apocalyptic disaster dared blow her way.

The Bangladeshi kept ribbing the Pakistani. He was not able to digest Ali's physical closeness to his newly discovered love. How dare the chef potter with pans that were not his own? He tried to put him down by harping on his Pakistani-accented English.

'Oh, shut up!' Ali bellowed in flawless English.

'No, Ali,' Zeenat pitched in, upping the battle between her two suitors. 'What Shehzad wants you to acquire is the excruciatingly polite but obfuscatory speech of the true-blue Englishman.'

Rishi knew where this was headed for and jumped in with delight. 'She's right. An Englishman would never say, "Shut up!" He'll go like this: "Would you mind not speaking for a while?" Or more accurately, he'll put it ever so apologetically, "Actually, old chap, I really am sorry for making this dreadful demand, but if it were possible, would you please oblige me with a few moments of silence—if you can, that is? Thank you."'

And that brought the house down. The four of them rolled and rolled in splits at this supreme exhibition of the prim and proper English language, which was suffocatingly polite even when one intended to be rude.

'You're on point,' admitted the Bangladeshi dude, throwing up his hands in mock surrender.

'Yaar, you forgot one more thing they do,' Ali pointed out to his Indian mate lounging on the cushion. 'What about "Hmm . . . ah . . . um . . ." How can you . . . er . . . speak English like the English, without "um . . . er . . ." at least twenty times in every sentence?'

They again went berserk, exploding with laughter. They slapped Ali's back and were hugging, laughing and crying at the same time. Totally thrilled at the way Ali had blasted the English penchant for not coming straight to the point. Zeenat was getting cramps from laughing non-stop.

The night was still young. Ali, Shehzad and Zeenat lingered in the living room, drinking coffee and talking. Rishi had retired to his room early. He needed to finish some work, he told them. Ali got busy trying every possible antic to woo his lady love. Shehzad's eyes ordered him to buzz off, but there seemed to be network issues, his message was not getting delivered. He watched the Lahori lion prowling round and round his girl, roaring poetry that complimented her looks, her walk, her hair, her words . . . dammit, everything!

'Leave something for me, you bastard,' Shehzad muttered under his breath.

Zeenat soaked up all the attention and adulation like she had been starved of it for centuries. Waltzing happily in this triangle of her own making, she thrived on this proxy tug of war waging across international waters. The Indian had the tact to play the mediator, but he had gone off to work, sleep or whatever he claimed he had to do behind closed doors. So she played games with these two, taking sides at random.

22

The agony uncle read that one mail again and again. It had a familiar ring to it. He couldn't quite place it, but it sent all his alarm bells going.

'When life dumps you again and again, should you blame the world or yourself for being this stupid?'

He replied with care, 'Not stupid. It's coz you're strong that life tests you and not the people around you.'

'He who advises you so, when he himself dumps you, then?' A reader had suddenly appeared on live chat and took him head-on.

God, it was her! From a new email ID now. No wonder he'd been getting those vibes. And she was right—he had dumped her by immersing himself in the lives and issues of other readers. He had forsaken her after pledging forever support. Well, that was because he needed time to attend to his other readers. He could not ignore them forever—this was his job. But then, if he knew not how to manage his time, that was not her problem! Like you looked before leaping, should you not assess before you promise? Also, his crime was graver than that of the average guy who dumps. He had let go of the one girl who helped him reflect on his own insecurities and fears. She had showed him, in full Technicolor, what he had shut his eyes to all this time. Introduced him to the Rishi he was—a zombie. Living in denial. Just like her.

How could he have let go of her? Weren't they fighting the same losing battle? Caving in to their diminished self-esteem? All that bravado of not wanting anything or anyone, he realized, had been just a mask. His battle had been mostly with his own self, like she was warring within, destroying herself and her notions of family. Rejected by the world, both had withdrawn into themselves and become their own punching bags.

Her cries of pain had awakened him to his own sorrow. Her misgivings rivalled the misconceptions he had long nurtured. The two tales were tragic, with most of their wounds self-inflicted. They were truly similar, so her pain became his own.

The agony uncle shook his head in despair. Typing furiously, he reached out to her again, wanting to reconnect with her and himself. He told her about his intense, but failed affair. They shared notes, laughed and cried together, not judging each other. She loved dewdrops she told him. He hated standing in a queue, he confided.

'Will you adopt me?'

He was flummoxed by her question. 'Don't you already have a foster family?' He asked her this, for he knew not how one could possibly adopt a soulmate.

Soulmate? When had she become that? What was going on? He was discovering new stuff by the minute. Her words seemed to be pinging his brain, making him see not just himself but even his feelings anew. But wait a minute—wasn't *he* supposed to be the agony uncle? What the hell was she doing, ministering his agonies! This girl was one big jigsaw. She puzzled him even as she helped him solve his own riddles.

'I got no family—real or foster. Yesterday or today.' Her reply nailed him.

He accepted her then in whichever way she wanted him to. 'So you'll be mine from now on—legally, illegally, in every possible way.' A smiley was all he got in return and then, poof! She had gone offline. Dammit! That's how it was in the virtual world. Relationships were forged and broken and even frozen with a click. Rishi left his chair to lounge on the bed and daydream about his new adoptee. Family member, not adoptee. Adoption was a dirty word, so she had said.

Two delicious hours later, he went back to his desk and mails. A fifty-year-old woman wanted to remarry but the only real offer she'd got involved her becoming a co-wife. She liked this guy, she said, but he had two more wives and would be visiting her on a rota if they married. He told her to see how much time and emotional resources she had available before taking a call. If she was high on career and short on time, and not averse to the idea of having a part-time man, what the heck, go ahead, he counselled.

Another reader wanted him to provide a checklist that he could tick off before getting engaged to a girl. The fellow also wanted top ten rules for a happy marriage. The agony uncle took pains to draft a structured response to this very systematic query. 'Life has a way of surprising you that defies all planning,' he wrote back. 'When the heart gets struck, it punctures every list and rule in the head or paper. So plan, but be prepared to have to chuck that plan,' he advised sagely.

The next mail in his inbox was a job offer. It had been waiting since yesterday and offered to pay nearly double of what he was getting now. An unputdownable offer that also involved frequent travel to Edinburgh, Inverness and other Scottish towns. What more could an applicant with his sort of CV ask for?

Rishi's first thought was it had to be a prank. But who could it be? Well, the world was full of sadists, who got their kicks taking the wind out of people. Must be one of those jerks, he figured. So he checked out the company profile, visiting their website, zoomed in on the careers page . . . and found to his shock that all was okay. Could the mail actually be genuine? His eyes widened in wonder. Should he call and check once? He didn't want to make an ass of himself. But what if it was real! He needed to find out for sure. Swinging between yes and no, he finally made that call in the morning and experienced a huge shot in the arm. The email was real—they did want him and that too, immediately!

Rishi hung up in a daze. He had learnt to deal with pain and failure. But success? He was clueless there . . . it was new territory for him. He would have to invest in some new suits probably for those sales trips up north, and arrange for Ali to water his bonsai. Yes, he did have one, though he never liked to discuss or even acknowledge it, unlike the English always going on and on about their gardens and cats!

And yes, he would also need to resign from *Desi Beats*. He couldn't ditch the column overnight, would have to manage it somehow for a month at least. Then let go. *Let go* . . . there were those words again, springing up twice in a day. Telling him that he was not doing right. What was going on? He didn't want to let go, was that it?

But this offer had come as a big climb-up. And didn't he find out only today that he no longer wanted to hang around like a zombie. He wanted to live, not stagnate. And rising up the ranks was surely a part of living. Yet, there were parts of him that objected to this good fortune. Not liking this windfall. Not ready to let it blow him away. He had just found his feet and it wouldn't do to get carried away, not even by a wave that promised success.

Rishi made up his mind. He decided to stay grounded, rooted to his new reality, a reality built around her. A smile lit up his face, announcing a ceasefire. No conflicting emotions, his heart had won—a heart that now beat with *Desi Beats* and all that he had found there. His head nodded in understanding—having calculated that it could not operate optimally or even logically when it was too full of another person.

He sat up straighter at his desk and sent a graceful rejection to the handsome offer, telling them how pleased and honoured he was to be given this opportunity of a lifetime. But regretting that this unique opportunity presented itself at an inopportune moment, so he had to refuse it with more than a twinge of disappointment.

That done, the agony uncle got back to work again, opening the next reader email. It was a lonely, middle-aged lady this time who was sick of meeting douchebags. She inquired, 'Are there men who could keep a clean and tidy house and entertain her suitably over the weekends?' He read it with a smile and answered with another. There were a lot of nice men out there, he assured her—ones who could fill her lonesome moments in many different ways. Some may even vacuum her place as well to save on rent, but he could not be certain if they would not be entertaining more than one lady over the week. Pressing the 'send' button, he felt satisfied and at home. This was what he wanted to do, not be a slave to pound notes. Fifteen more mails to go, then he could switch over to her.

She had pinged him, reappearing as suddenly as she had disappeared. She would wait for him to finish, she told him. The agony uncle looked anything but agonized as he went about finishing his chores. A stupid smile sat on his face as he typed. Someone was waiting for him. That was enough to give him a high.

23

Not only his begum, now even Mullah was taken with him. The whole night he had thought of just one person. This said a lot about a person who had slept soundly even on his wedding night. This tormentor of his sleep also happened to be his tenant, and now, Mullah planned to offer the bugger a lease of a lifetime. He couldn't wait for the dawn to break. The first ray of sun to break across the horizon had him up and about and itching to summon his prize catch.

* * *

'Ali!' thundered the landlord on the phone.

The chef rubbed his eyes, half asleep, his ears registering a familiar, threatening voice.

'Ali!' This was louder, awakening Ali to the reality of him having a landlord and the necessity of being respectful to him, no matter what bleeding hour the man chose to make his presence felt.

'Ji, janaab.' Ali was courteous even when only half awake.

His gracious tone warmed the heart of the old curmudgeon. He had been right and his begum too had not led him up the wrong path this time. This fellow was perfect—exactly what he was looking for.

The line had gone silent. Had the Mullah gone to sleep? Why did he call then? Must have been a mistake. Or had he called in his sleep, like that neighbour in Lahore, who would sleepwalk every other night? These British sure do strange things, and Mullah was no less British now.

'I want you to come over to my place now,' Mullah bellowed, resurrecting like a phoenix from a line that Ali believed had gone dead.

It scared him stiff. When your landlord calls you at 7 a.m. and orders you to come show your face, your life was definitely screwed. Cursing in chaste Urdu, Ali wore whatever was handy, threw the three pieces of kaju burfi from last night's dinner into a box—they would be his olive branch if the landlord was breathing fire—and mumbling a prayer, went to meet his fate.

He did not have to walk far. Five houses down, he saw the landlord zoom up to him. 'Meeting trouble halfway . . .' muttered Ali as he whipped up a sweet smile to greet Mullah. And he got a sweeter one in return. That floored him completely. A sweeter-than-honey smile on Mullah's face looked as fake as purple chutney on a tikka. What did the crafty demon want at this goddamn hour! Ali was getting edgy now.

'Son,' began Mullah, gathering his tenant in a bear hug that wrung the life out of him and flattened the burfis too. It wasn't the physical act that took the wind out of Ali—it was pure shock that did him in. Like a wooden doll, the chef hung out there, ready to be beaten, grilled or charred.

'Let's take a walk.'

Feeling exactly like a lamb on its way to halal, Ali fell in step the second Mullah commanded.

They had not crossed three houses when Mullah cleared his throat and asked, 'What you think of Zeenat?'

'Zeenat . . .?' blabbered Ali. 'Why, nothing!'

Had this old fox zoomed into his heart? Ali was positively shaking now. He'd be slaughtered in this foreign land and no one would know or care. The bastard would even deny him a funeral. Love could be so painfully final. Had Ali known, he would've cooked his heart and served it to the dogs before it dared beat for the landlord's daughter.

'You don't like her?' Mullah was so excruciatingly direct.

Ali only nodded a no. He had lost his voice.

Mullah took the nod to mean ayes. *Ah!* That's what he'd thought. The boy was smitten but shy. 'So how do we go about it?' It was a matter-of-fact question.

But the answer was as evasive as Ali could make it. 'Let's not do anything about it.' It had taken every ounce of his Pathani guts to muster that reply.

Mullah went both black and white at once. Thundering black in anger at the lethargy of this generation when it came to taking things to their logical conclusion. And pale white at the thought of his daughter losing such an appropriate partner. 'Look, I'll make it good for you,' Mullah offered. 'Everything. I'll take care of everything.'

Ali stole a confused look at him. How on earth could someone kill him and make it good for him too? Unless it was a life insurance agent gifting him a policy that his beloved heir could make a killing from after Mullah killed him. But he had no heir, beloved or otherwise. So the point of this offer escaped him.

Scratching his un-shampooed hair, Ali felt jittery and irritated with the world.

'You take my Zeenat, and I'll take care of you.' There, he had got it off his chest. Put it bluntly to the Pakistani who was dilly-dallying.

'Take Zeenat?' Ali repeated in a daze. 'Where?'

'You had too much to drink last night, son?' Mullah threw his prospective son-in-law a look that probed for more signs of a hangover. 'It's okay now, but when Zeenat's around, mind it. You'll need to control. Else she'll end up drinking double of you.'

Ali's head was finally clearing. Mullah was clearly not out to kill him, not in the way he had imagined. Instead, this had something to do with Zeenat. His Zeenat. And Mullah's Zeenat. The landlord wanted to send her somewhere with him. Mashallah, what an opportunity! He needed more information.

'No . . . no. I'm fine, janaab. Even Zeenat is . . . even she did not drink last night.'

Mullah's face broke into a smile. 'Ah! So that's where she was last night—I should've known!' He patted the Pakistani with affection.

Shit! Ali swore. Why had he let on that Zeenat had been with them? What if that was her secret? She would not forgive him for bleating it out. *God!* He felt so sheepish.

'See, I have only one daughter,' Mullah started again, 'and it's natural that I want the best for her.'

Ali nodded, desperate to know where this was heading.

'If you keep her well, I'll do everything for you. Your . . .'

'No . . . no. You don't have to do anything, janaab,' Ali butted in to reassure. 'We all love having her with us.'

'All?'

Mullah picked on that one word. Clearly, there was a communication problem here. Either he was not making his point clearly or this boy had been drinking and lying about it.

'If you marry her, I'll . . .'

'Marry!' Ali jumped, his ears burning. Now, it was Ali's turn to think that the other had had a bit too much to drink the previous night.

'You don't want to marry her?' Mullah stopped to check.

Ali halted too, his jaw open and mind numb.

'In that case,' said Mullah, 'this conversation is pointless. Let's go back.'

Ali gripped Mullah's hand as he turned to walk off. Stuttering, he began, 'I . . . I . . . I don't know what to say.'

Seeing a glimmer of hope, Mullah restated his offer. 'If you marry my girl, I'll give you whatever you came here for.'

That sounded like a promise. And Ali knew Mullah honoured his promises.

'Haji's Hotel, isn't it?' Mullah asked.

Ali looked stricken. Was the landlord owning his mind too now?

'Come on, tell me,' he goaded. The chef was shy, he knew. In fact, that was one of the things both Fiza and he liked about the chap.

Ali nodded again. It was doubtful he would get his voice back again today.

'Just think. You get Zeenat and also your hotel. It's a deal.'

The way Mullah put it, it did sound like a clapper of a deal. Only Ali wanted her even if there was no deal, but mashallah, if he was getting his dhaba back too, nothing could be better. Glowing, Ali agreed to all that Mullah was offering.

'Don't just keep nodding,' the prospective father-in-law admonished his to-be son-in-law. 'Go! Propose to her.'

That was the dicey part. While the offer had him dancing, the thought of executing it, starting with a proposal, made Ali sweat profusely.

Mullah saw this and egged him on. 'Don't let someone beat you to this.'

Shehzad! Ali thought of him at once, and his heart went cold. Mullah was right. He had to cook this one right away! Shehzad was on the prowl, salivating. Ali couldn't let him make the first move. Especially not now.

24

Rishi was floating from one cloud to the next, bouncing from exhilaration to euphoria, feeling energetic and fidgety. Restless and on the edge, not hungry, not thirsty, and only shivering—with delight, with anxiety. His heartbeat kept rising and his breathing became faster, riding anticipation and sometimes, panic. He was scared about the direction in which he was headed. But she was there with him, in those clouds, in this new world, ruling his mind, living in those mails. Writing. Replying. Chatting. Living it up in the virtual world. The two building their own alternative reality up there, with just a user name and password, and profiles created especially for each other.

They spoke of everything under the sun. One day it was on the uselessness of religion. Another day it was about fantasies and algorithms. Actually, it was Rishi who brought up algorithms, when they were talking of random stuff that people liked.

'This Chinese dude I dated had a baked beans fetish.'

'Baked beans?'

'Yeah. Bread, salad, fruit, noodles—he topped everything with beans.'

'Seriously?'

'I left before he threw them on me too!'

'Good you canned him!'

And they laughed at his doublespeak. In their rooms, before their separate screens, but totally connected.

Rishi hadn't felt so free for a long time. Passing by his room, Shehzad's ears pricked up at the unfettered laughter. Curiosity got the better of him and he barged in, not bothering to knock. His antenna went up seeing the Indian freaking out on his laptop. Rishi was having fun! Rishi! He crept closer to peek and got a bird's eye view of the cosy chat.

'Aah! Lovey dovey, are we?'

Rishi shot the Bangladeshi a look that dripped venom.

'You're so right,' crooned Shehzad, repeating what he'd read on the screen.

Rishi chased him out, swearing at him in all the three languages he knew. That Bangladeshi vermin, he would shred his reputation in seconds now. But there were some things you just couldn't control. So he stopped thinking about Shehzad and got back to her. She brought out a side in him no one here had seen. Even he hadn't for quite some time.

'And these Brit boys, they just don't want to grow up!'

Rishi was all eyes and ears. Pages from her life were flickering online.

'You don't like them?'

'I do. But all they like is to get smashed in parks on cheap cider.'

That was exactly what Rishi too had found; he began to feel like he was talking to himself. He shared an early memory with her. 'When I first got here, I'd gone to a house party—saw these teenagers bouncing around in circles! It was so dumb. Two or three years younger, they were. But made me feel I was back in kindergarten.'

She had danced at countless such parties, she confided, and found them equally juvenile.

'I can change this if you want.' Rishi was treading with infinite care now. Every word he typed had a purpose.

'How?' she asked.

'You went eyes shut till now and got these wrong numbers.'

'So?'

'I can give you an algorithm that finds you the perfect match.'

'Algorithm?' He had lost her there.

'It's basic maths. You put in your choices and the set formula gives you the right match for your input.'

'Don't go technical on me.'

'I won't.' He backtracked with haste, not wanting to lose her.

'Okay, what input do you want?'

She was game. His pulse beat faster and louder. 'Tell me your taste in men.'

'What you want to know?'

'What you dig most: looks, brains, humour or sex?'

'Fun. He should be fun.'

'And?'

'And . . . he should . . . he should know how to see inside me. And talk to me—laugh with me.'

'You want someone you can be yourself with?'

'Yes. That's it. Someone I can bare my soul to.'

Rishi's hands became clammy. What she wanted was what he had to offer. The agony uncle had been peeking into her soul, putting her insides in order. Even now they were sharing, talking, laughing—just what she sought. Only, the agony uncle no longer felt avuncular. This was a different track they were on.

Rishi's fingers trembled as he typed in a response to her input. 'My algorithm tells me, your input matches our output.'

Things went dead quiet at her end. Not a single character was typed.

'Mostly.'

It was he who added this one word to fill the gap. Trying to be specific and true. And at the same time, praying she understood him and accepted this thing that was developing between them. He hoped they could figure it out without another agony aunt or uncle wedging in between to sort out their mess.

The screen remained blank and silent.

'You there?'

His heart was in his mouth as he typed this with shaky fingers. But she hadn't signed off—yet.

'I am.'

He sent her an emoji then. And another. And another. More and more. No single emoji could express all that he was going through now. Trepidation. Nerves. Confusion. Vacuum. Anticipation. Hope. Fear. And finally, relief at her confirming that she was still there.

All was not lost. While she was there, there was a glimmer of a new tomorrow. Yes, Rishi had now learnt to jump past failures and hold on to every silver lining. It was her magic that made him this way.

She reverted with a smiley and a comment, 'So complex you are.'

That was for his army of emoticons, each different from the other. 'Simplify me,' he requested, bolstered by her smiley.

'I am powerless from behind a screen.'

Rishi's jaw fell open. Was that . . . an invitation? Was she suggesting . . . meeting offline? Actually, meet? His life was becoming quite a T20 match. One never knew which way it would swing.

High on confidence, he typed, 'Show me your powers offline then.'

She went quiet again. She was probably thinking—debating.

'You got those powers, don't you?' he baited her.

And she called his bluff. 'Don't pull your dude act on me. I'm no shrinking wallflower.'

'I already know that.'

That took them on a new track. She wanted to know what made him so sure of her. What if she was a lying octogenarian with dyed hair and a dozen facelifts?

'You'll still be young at heart and on the same wavelength as me.'

That went bullseye, hitting her exactly where it mattered. But she still kept fishing, 'I can airbrush my pictures, but not my face. Can you live with it?'

She was playing with him, he knew. He liked it and so he played along. 'I'll iron away your wrinkles. Have you smiling naughty at me—at all times.'

He had her then.

'What time tomorrow?'

Her response was too sudden for him to react suitably.

'You checking your calendar?' She was getting impatient; that was a good sign.

'You just caught me unawares. Got no calendar.'

'See you aware and alert 5 p.m. tomorrow.'

That tickled him. Her sense of humour was insane and inane, just like his.

'On which moon?'

'The one that shines over Holborn Tube station.'

'Do we eat and drink? Or am I to feast on you only?'

'See you by the coffee vending machine, smart-arse. Don't be late.'

'Send me your picture. I don't want to eat the wrong girl.'

'Your heart will find me. It should—if you got one.'

'Point taken. Tomorrow then.'

She signed off before he did. Girls! And their damn attitude! But he knew how to handle it, the agony uncle that he was. A pro in matters of the heart.

25

Ali read and reread the instructions on the packet—he wanted to get it right. It would knock the wind out of his lady love. He had seen her fingering that Dhakai dope's tattoo. It choked his heart every time she did that. No more of it now. He'd give her one that was exclusively hers to play with—on his left arm, etched there just for her. He had ordered a handsome lion design. It came last night with complete instructions: 'Paste on flat areas with no body hair.'

For the first time in his life, Ali eyed the thick jungle sprouting on his hands and legs with irritation. Daintily, he pasted his lion tattoo sticky side down, over his ample and hairy bicep. He had cut out the sticker with great care, scissoring neatly right next to the image border. But not even love could force him to shave away his body hair. Peeling off the cover, he admired the magnificent beast now stuck on to him, and puffed up with pride, like he'd got the big cat for real. This would be his Valentine's Day gift to her. She'd fall prey to it for sure.

Now, only to book her for the evening. Ali had planned meticulously and even got another cook to fill in for him at work. As for wooing her, he decided to copy Shehzad's style because that seemed to work on her. So Ali checked out this party boat sailing the Thames under the starry night sky, beckoning lovers to reserve early. They served alcohol, and you could pop on your headphones—like they did the other day—and dance the night away. It was guaranteed to melt your date. Allah willing, he would have snagged an 'Inglish' begum for himself by tomorrow. Pulling his T-shirt sleeve down gingerly to cover his lion, which still felt a tad sticky, Ali counted the notes in his wallet and marched out to the kitchen to make himself some elaichi chai. Then off to Mullah's pad to invite her in person.

* * *

Shehzad had felt gutted when she went back to Mullah. They had a roof here too, one that Mullah only owned. If it was okay for her to camp here one night, why not more nights too? And why had she parked herself on the sofa that night? What was suddenly wrong with his bed? She had been in it enough to know it was more comfortable than the bloody sofa. With Zeenat, he was always floundering. Just when he thought he understood her, she became someone else! Acted totally insane, and drove him nuts too.

But hey, why was he ranting! Today was special. Fourteenth of February came just once a year. Zeenat had invaded his heart and now it was his turn to attack. Seduce her with his charming routine—copy Kanye West, perhaps.

But heck, no. He could not hire a whole damn stadium like that moneybags. And set up gigantic screens everywhere to pop the big question. With him, the only fireworks would be in the bed and the orchestra would blare through his mini Bose speakers. Not that he was planning to sidestep the romance—he'd take her to that pub overlooking the river at Hammersmith. And later, they could hold hands, and neck on the park benches overlooking the Thames. Something had gone woozy in him—he actually felt like doing this tonight.

* * *

Mullah snapped at the Pakistani ringing the doorbell. 'I told you to play the hero, not the cop.'

Ali looked blank.

'She's left.'

'What?'

'What, my foot! If you land late, like the bloody police always do in the movies, some smart-arse will whisk her away.'

'She's gone . . .'

Ali looked so deflated that Fiza was overcome with pity for him. So she hollered past her husband's shoulder, 'I overheard her telling someone she was going to the British Museum.'

'British Museum?'

'Go. . . . go, while there is still time,' said Mullah, toning down his irritation, for the kid looked stricken. Had he chosen rightly for his baby? Why was this fellow so slow? Mullah himself had pounced on Fiza right away. This guy needed to act fast.

Ali did a U-turn and walked back to where he had come from. He shouldn't have wasted time over tea. Why the hell did he have to sit and sip! His bird had flown and he had no idea how or where to catch her! And what about the boat ride? Should he book or should he wait? Feeling annoyed, he rolled up his sleeves, swiped back the hair crowding his sweaty forehead and stomped inside, his mood muddy and muddled.

At once, someone tapped his elbow and thrust it upward, taking him totally by surprise. Was he being mugged? Inside his house? How was that possible? When Ali calmed down a bit, he found his lion being examined, inch by bloody inch, by a pair of Bangladeshi eyes that were growing bigger and more impudent by the second.

'Wow!' Knocked for a six by what he saw, Shehzad exclaimed loudly, the sticker lion tickling him no end. Finally, letting go of the stuck-on tattoo, the Dhakai douchebag went hysterical, holding on to his sides as he convulsed against the wall. Ali knew it was the stick-on lion that had Shehzad cracking up. With a tug, he pulled down his sleeve, seething at this breach of privacy. But it was too late. The bastard had seen what he wasn't meant to, and now he would eat him alive. Mullah was bloody right. He must learn to do stuff in time.

'Sticky, fucking . . . paper cat!'

Shehzad's tongue had gone wild now, and how he mocked Ali for his sticker tattoo till every vein in him bristled with irritation.

'Kinda cute it is,' Shehzad pronounced with mock seriousness. 'Almost as sweet as you, mate. So sugary and . . .'

He didn't get to finish. Ali elbowed him in the stomach, sending him flying back to the wall. He had fed this tummy enough—it was time to rip it open. Going mad, the Pakistani hit Shehzad left and right, connecting wherever he could with a wrath that defied all sense. Not that the Bangla boy took it all lying down. Once he'd got over the suddenness of this attack, he retaliated with equal recklessness, escalating the skirmish to a full-blown battle, and things around them went flying.

The noise had Rishi rushing out of his room. Had the Irish Republican Army finally invaded England? But this was different—and looked far more deadly. His two housemates were trying to clobber each other to death and doing a darn good job of it. The Indian's first instinct was to jump in the middle and announce a drinks break, but his brain stopped him in time. The chances of him surviving were barely 10 per cent. So he did what he felt was the next best choice in the circumstances—he called Zeenat, gave her a war synopsis and then put her on the speakerphone.

She tamed both the gladiators on the phone in less than a millisecond.

'Don't do this to me. You guys are all I have. Don't. Please. Mullah's hurt me so much—you can't. Else . . .'

That unsaid threat did it. Ali's punch stopped mid-air. Shehzad pulled out of whatever he was going to do next. Rishi heaved an audible sigh of relief. His house and the world were safe once more.

Thanking Zeenat who had already hung up on them, he got back to buttoning up his shirt. Sloppy Rishi was dressing with care today. A crisp, olive-green full-sleeve shirt made him look dapper. Dark trousers held in place with his favourite belt. About to spray some cologne, he checked himself in time. Those housemates of his would sniff out his secret in no time, and blow it to galactic size and rib him till doomsday. No, he couldn't risk it with these lunatics! Just a wee bit, pleaded his heart. So he ended up spraying some anyway.

Ali and Shehzad had no date to dress up for. Remembering it was Valentine's Day, Shehzad had got up at noon and dialled Zeenat. She told him to call back later or tomorrow.

Tomorrow! He couldn't postpone Valentine's just because
she had got it in that head of hers to visit a damn museum
today. But he couldn't tell her as much, not on the phone
at least. She would smell something fishy instantly and fire
off a hundred and one questions. Why should they meet on
Valentine's Day? What was he trying to say? Hell! He wanted
to declare his love in person. Not on some damn phone line.
So he decided to wait.

Slamming his door shut, Ali at once tugged up his sleeve
to check if his lion was okay. To his relief, like the ad had
promised, it was a quality product. The sticker showed no
sign of wear or tear after his battle. The predator still prowled
magnificently on his bicep, firing him up for the evening
ahead. Taking a one-minute shower, he changed into his
best outfit—he had bought only this one set since arriving
in London—and in front of the mirror practised the lines he
would say to her. In ten minutes, he was ready and outside
the front door, debating whether to take the Tube or the bus.

He saw Rishi inside a cab, instructing the driver where
to take him. Ali was about to ask where the Indian was going
when someone whizzed past him and hopped into the cab
beside Rishi. It was that idiot, Shehzad. Again, he had left him
gaping! Ali swore he won't be beaten this time and raced up
to Rishi's window to pile in if the cab was headed his way.

'Holborn,' said Rishi before Ali could ask.

What the hell! These guys never let him get in a word,
thought the Pakistani.

'And Shehzad's getting off at the British Museum,' Rishi
added.

Ali went cold. She was meeting this tattooed twit at the
museum! Mullah had warned him against exactly this type of a
scenario. But he never thought it would be Shehzad. The guy

was a joke. True, she too fooled around with him sometimes. But this Bangladeshi pest was mostly piling on to her and she was too polite to shoo him off. He'd change all that tonight.

'Ali! You're keeping the cab waiting,' screamed Rishi, cutting into Ali's reverie.

The Pakistani, to their shock, got in as well, squeezing in at the back without saying a word.

'Brick Lane?' Rishi quizzed, wondering why Ali was leaving so early for work.

'Hmm . . .' Ali only grunted, not too sure he could control himself if he opened his mouth.

* * *

Shehzad had not a thought to spare for the Pakistani. The last half-hour had been hectic. He'd got this brainwave to not wait for Zeenat's call, but to surprise her instead. He'd land up at the museum, a place where she would never dream of seeing even the ghost of Shehzad. He would catch her unawares and zap her with his truth. Bare his heart before the art of the world. His drama queen would lap it up. This was what her idol—Shah Rukh Khan—would do. He would lean back, spread out his arms and declare his love, unabashedly, in front of the whole world. If SRK could do that, he could do one better. So he'd wiggled into his black Calvin Klein jeans, slid into that tight T-shirt she particularly liked, slicked back his hair and jumped out. Something nagged him as he reached the front door. A gift! Girls dig gifts. Dammit, he wasn't the flowers-and-chocolates type. There wasn't any time anyway. He had to reach fast before she wandered off somewhere else. Would have to snatch something from the house only. But what?

Shehzad walked back into his room, and finding nothing, circled the hall, the kitchen, and then stopped at the fridge as usual. And there, he got his second brainwave. He'd give her that plastic heart that had come in the box of cereal they bought the other day. The pack had been a special promo offer for Valentine's Day—at a steal along with a two-inch-wide glowing plastic heart. He sure knew how to use that toy heart, how to pop it to her.

Sneaking rings inside cakes and wine glasses were old hat. He'd place his plastic heart inside something way more tempting. Shehzad opened the fridge, took out one of Ali's yummy kebabs, stuffed the freebie heart into its spicy filling, sealed it up good and proper, wrapped it in foil and pocketed it just in time. He heard Rishi come out and head straight for the kitchen. The fellow was dressed to go somewhere. Not to work, definitely, deduced Shehzad. Saw him guzzle down a whole bottle of water. That seemed curious too. But he had too much on his mind to dwell on Rishi for long. His gift arranged, he bounced to the front door, halting there suddenly to ask Rishi which way he was going and how.

'Holborn. By cab.'

Smashing! The British Museum wasn't far from there. The Indian, surprisingly, had booked a cab, which made it perfect for him to hitch a ride. Into the cab he jumped before his housemate, looking mighty pleased at the way things were aligning with his wishes. Even the Indian smelt good today, and had dressed fancily too. What was up! Shehzad bit his tongue lest he tease Rishi to the point of irritation and lose this free cab ride. It hit him then that he'd forgotten to spray some of that stuff on himself, and today was special! Shehzad jumped out of the cab, shouting out to Rishi he'd be back in less than a second. He did return in a flash, bolting past Ali, who he did not see standing by the cab.

Crammed in the cab, Ali cursed Shehzad. He ground his teeth at the thought of the Bangladeshi hovering near his soon-to-be begum. Perched next to him, Shehzad was tickled by the fact that this Pakistani's kebab was to play a leading role in his romance that evening. If only the dumb-ass knew, his head would burn like an overdone kebab. What a tasty thought! The Bangladeshi's smile got wider and wicked.

Oblivious to these two, Rishi was lost in his new world. It revolved round her, shone with her light, and was ready to embrace the darkness if that was what she chose to bestow. Saint Valentine kept a watch on his minions from up there, in the clouds, enjoying the foreplay of emotions before the rocking night ahead. Things were bound to get explosive!

26

It was a busy intersection and absolutely hell at peak times. Rishi glanced at his watch. It was almost 5 p.m. He rushed towards the one and only entrance at the Holborn tube station. These pricks had delayed him by fifteen minutes—Ali being indecisive and not getting off at Brick Lane and choosing to go to Covent Garden at the last minute. So much time he took to get his ass off the cab, glowering at Shehzad as he did so, not realizing that his juvenile antics were costing Rishi time and money.

And then that Dhaka Casanova insisted on being dropped off at the British Museum first. Hell, Rishi had booked the cab and would be the one paying for it, not that jerk. Yet the bugger had the balls to order him about. Thankfully, he had slipped out fast enough once the cab neared the museum gate. What had piqued his interest in art and sculpture overnight was another mystery, one that Rishi did not have the bandwidth to solve today. Let the fellow torture stone and canvas for a while! The world would be safer with the lampooning demon safely enclosed within the museum walls—at least Ali would be. Even someone blind could see how the Bangladeshi got the Pakistani's goat every time the two came within shouting distance. Shaking his head, Rishi shrugged off all thought of his housemates, and hurried inside to meet his fate.

Ali looked for a bus the minute he hopped off the cab—Covent Garden had never been his destination. But he didn't want that inked swine to know he was following him to the museum. The next bus was some five minutes away, so Ali decided to walk it. It wouldn't take him more than ten minutes. Shehzad did have a head start on him, being in the cab, but it is the turtle that eventually wins the race, he told himself. Was it the turtle or the tortoise? Ali wasn't sure. Whatever!

Shehzad reached the museum almost fifteen minutes before Ali, but the place was so huge that the Bangladeshi was going mad looking for his girl. He'd known it would be a spread, but he'd never thought there would be so many rooms and troops of visitors ambling in and out of every one of these rooms! To add to the clutter, school groups were crawling all over the place. It would be easier to find Zeenat in a haystack than this monstrosity of a place. He sighed in despair—the stuff that love made you do!

He was at the Montague Place entrance now; this area seemed more crowded because it was the entry to the Egyptian exhibits, housing mystical mummies and the preserved pharaohs—who belonged to Egypt, but got transported to museums all over the world so that they could be gawked at by the Americans, Asians and Europeans. A hushed awe filled the room housing these popular exhibits. Shehzad sped past historical and contemporary humans, looking for his love, and found an equally rare gem—a mummified crocodile! That transfixed him for a full five minutes.

Regaining control, he left the bewitching beauty and zoomed past the Great Court, turned left, sparing a scant glance at the Elgin Marbles, and moved on. She was nowhere. The Rosetta Stone was around, as was the Sutton Hoo Helmet and Clarence's Truck. But there was no Zeenat. He had checked the upper, ground and even the lower floors at a speed that would have been illegal on the roads. The museum was about to close and the visitors were filing out. Security was nudging any lingering fans firmly towards the exit. Shehzad was now at his wits' end. He'd even scanned the cafeteria and the gift shops. But his lady love eluded him.

Forty minutes of this museum hunt, however, won him a shocking jackpot. Ali! The paper lion was wandering around the atrium, peering into faces, corners, rooms and god knew what else till he spotted Shehzad, at almost the exact second that Shehzad spotted him—and came to a dead halt. Amidst this exodus, the Pakistani stood immobile, glowering at the Bangladeshi for leading him on this cat-and-mouse chase, on a day that was so important to him. And where was she? Ali's eyes panned the space surrounding the damn tattoo-cake frantically, came back to his face for a hint of what he sought, but drew a blank everywhere. Had the smart-arse hidden her somewhere? Or was he planning to run away with her, duping both Mullah and him? Shehzad was really raising his blood pressure way too much today.

Shehzad thought he was hallucinating. What was the Lahori doing here—the museum was the unlikeliest of places for him to be prowling in. And today of all days! Hadn't he got off at Covent Garden. Why was he here then? And if he needed to be here, why did he get down there? Shehzad cursed—things were getting too complicated, and it was getting late. The place was shutting and there was no sign of her yet. *Zeenie, where are you?*

It hit him then—this animal must've known she was coming here and so was prowling in a territory that was not his own, in a bid to win a prize that was beyond his station. It would serve him right to have someone else make off with her, that too, using a kebab he had made. As he savoured this evil thought, Shehzad felt his pocket to check his yummy heart was still there. Confirming its presence, he moved towards the exit, avoiding Ali, who fixed on him a deadly stare.

'Where's she?' roared Ali, drawing near.

'Scat!'

Spitting out that one word, Shehzad went his way, wanting to blot out his ape of a housemate from his vision and reality. But got collared back and found himself confronting the very reality he had chosen to obliterate.

'What've you done to Zeenat?' The beast was shaking as he demanded an answer from Shehzad.

What made Ali so sure that Zeenat was here? Even as Shehzad seethed at being manhandled by this wild Pakistani, his brain was working overtime. How did he know? Was it . . . no . . . it couldn't be . . . no . . . hell, was Zeenat actually meeting up with this ape here? Had she totally lost it? Shehzad knew girls did really dumb things sometimes, but dating Ali? You had to be completely insane. He looked up at his snarling housemate with wonder and distaste, trying to see what Zeenat could've seen.

Ali had had enough of this rat—that lion jibe still hurt, and now he'd hidden his girl too! How dare he strut around as if nothing had happened? Ali would break his every bone and make him squeal. He had seen only the sunny side of him. But Ali could get dark and dangerous when needed. Swearing, Ali scruffed him by the collar and edged him close. The fellow had the balls to stare back at him. Now, what was he eyeing him for? Was he . . .

He suddenly let go of Shehzad like he'd been stung. Ali wanted to finish off what he'd started but a man in uniform was looking at them from afar, so he reined in his temper. Shehzad stood up straight and brushed his collar with a swagger meant to irritate.

Shehzad saw the security guard too and sneered. *Good!* Let this buffoon bake behind bars. That would show Zeenat what trash she was mixing with.

'Where is Zeenat?' Ali ground out a second time, his hand clenching in a fist held back with much effort.

'Stop blabbering, arsehole!' Shehzad was losing patience now. Also, Zeenat was nowhere around. Had this bloody museum swallowed her up? Swearing, he punched the air, wanting to break that curved criss-crossing glass roof jeering at him from up there.

'Last time, I'm asking you . . .' began Ali, his eyes threatening the guy he had cooked for all these months.

'She's not a souvenir that I can pocket—use your overcooked brain sometimes.'

It was scathing, but logical. Ali began to see his point— the girl was truly missing. What was he to do now? He saw no path. His feet were aching with all that walking and searching, and his blood was still on the boil—all because of this rat!

'I'm looking for her too,' Shehzad admitted, looking goofy for once.

'What?' Ali was confused. What was this new act?

'She came to see you but . . .'

Before his housemate could answer, security was upon them. They didn't just want to throw the twosome out, but also question them first. Ali swore under his breath. This Bangla bomb fomented trouble wherever he went.

27

Rishi made a U-turn. No, it wasn't the escalator. They had decided to meet up at the coffee vending machine right outside. His brain was all fucked up today. Excitement, delay, the morons he lived with—together they had fried every neuron inside his skull.

Running now, lest she gave up on him, he headed for the Nescafé signage his eyes had picked up on the way. A few metres from the machine, he stopped with a jerk, bewitched by the beauty in the red jacket waiting right next to the machine. She'd messaged him earlier that day to say she'd be wearing crimson, changing her mind about playing cat-and-mouse with his heart. There she was, striking a pose in red! Voluptuous in the right measure, the air of mystery and magic surrounding her seduced him no end. Raven locks fell in a sheath, dancing past her shoulders, veiling her face. He inched closer to steal a look past the lush, black curtain. She turned to face him the same second.

Their eyes met. And held. And bulged. A zillion emotions sparked in both that one nanosecond. Shock. Disbelief. Denial. Confusion. Hesitation. Reservation.

Zeenat! Rishi's entire being rejected this reality completely. It couldn't be. There was definitely some mistake! A dreadful misunderstanding! Perplexed, he stared at her, not trusting his eyes. Surely, things had got mixed up. But she was wearing red and standing right there, next to the vending machine. Looking so hauntingly beautiful. Having the same misgivings as him.

Their eyes were on each other, reluctant, awkward, and yet, loathe to let go. It was as if each was seeing the other for the first time today. Trying to make sense of this twisted fate. In those few seconds, they swung between distrust and longing, rebuff and acceptance, from indifference to understanding, and finally, graduating to love. They covered so much ground and space. It was like they were building their own new world out there. The sea of humanity around them had long ceased to exist. It was only them and their battles. She did not budge from her post. He decided to take the first step. Dispelling anxious clouds and shy winds, floating on hope and courage, he pushed himself to take that first step, a giant one, into a whole new world.

Boom! The whole thing exploded. Blotting out his world, flattening him, plunging ice picks into his eardrums, flooding his lungs with smoke and dust. The force of the blast numbed his mind and body. Like a sucker punch, it hit him fast and hard, knocking him off the ground. And giving him no time to get a grip on what was happening till it was over. And then a sudden silence, a stillness that was unnerving. The vibrations rippled through him much later. Things were still shaking around him as he tried to take stock. Thick black-grey smoke swirled around. Shards of glass and bits of metal, paper and cloth were scattered everywhere.

Rishi staggered to his feet, wobbly and disoriented. He was having trouble seeing clearly and it felt like his ears had been stuffed with wads of cotton. He could taste the thick grit of smoke on his tongue and his lungs were burning. His head was spinning as he tried to make sense of what had happened. People were panicking, running back and forth, terror writ large on their flurrying bodies.

The acrid smell of smoke and death hung thick, overwhelming him. Covering his ears with his palms, Rishi opened his mouth to equalize the pressure. That he could think of doing this told him that his mind was more or less intact. Thank god! He looked at himself up and down, ensuring that all his limbs were still with him. And Zeenat! His next thought was of her.

She was gone but in that fraction of a second, the topography of the station had changed, death and destruction, chaos and fear were now everywhere. It was raw, palpitating fear. The bomb had not emptied the station yet. People were still hurrying out, escaping debris and smoke and sections that had caved in. He ran to join them, not to flee, but to search. He went looking for Zeenat—in every face, under every piece of rubble—wanting her to be safe, praying she was unscathed. His heart filled with dread with every passing minute. Had he lost her? Why did fate send her to him when it was going to take her away the next second? Was this his destiny?

He heard people shouting near the entrance. Rishi raced to check, it could be Zeenat. Pushing through men, women and clutter, he kept going, hurling ahead like a maniac, till he banged into a policeman coming his way. Gathering himself, not wasting time or effort to mumble an apology, he made to take off again, only to hit a wall—a human wall. A battery of uniforms had closed in on him in a sudden swoop, coming from left, right and behind him, making him fall down hard on his ass.

What an overreaction this was! An inadvertent banging into a cop and how these racist officers were avenging it! But yes, he should have said sorry. These Englishmen—they lived by their sorrys, thank yous and pleases. But how can one be polite during a bomb blast? It beat him. But one thing he learnt today—even the seemingly unruffled British could go hyper at times.

Sore all over, Rishi shrugged off his dark humour, held his back gingerly and started to get up. Balancing himself tenderly on one elbow, he raised his head, looking to push himself up sideways. And fell back in shock. A posse of cops had ringed him in a vicious circle; their eyes and body language told him something was bloody wrong. They weren't here to help, or wreak vengeance over a gentle collision. No. He was in deep shit! Deep, deep shit!

The police edged closer, ordered him to lie on his stomach, and turned him around at gunpoint, not giving him a second to process what was going on. Caked in dust, bleeding and hurt all over, he winced, but not in pain. More than agony, what he felt now was fear—terror. He was terrorized and wanted to scream that there had been some big mistake. Only he couldn't, for his mouth had gone dry and his senses were getting dulled. Something sharp had hit him somewhere in the back. These jokers surrounding him had immobilized him completely. He couldn't move or speak. He was losing focus. Swimming . . . the ground was swimming . . . bobbing up and down . . . and . . . sirens! Sirens were the last he heard of the audible world.

When he came to, he felt stiff, nauseous and filthy. Yanking up his arm, he made to wipe the dirt off his clammy face and got stuck. He couldn't raise the damn arm. Had he damaged it? The half-shut eyes were jolted wide open. He tried to swing his arm and failed. It was locked. Every nerve in him shuddered in shock as the mind struggled to grasp the horrendous fact that his arm had been locked behind him, cuffed to the left one, rigidly bound in metal.

Rishi went crazy then, jerking his arm up and down, trying to wrench free. But succeeded only in injuring his back. This was not real, it couldn't be. Why would they do this to him? There was nothing he could think of that he'd done to deserve this—nothing. Why then? Was there another Rishi Mathur in London, who'd whacked his mom-in-law or quartered his girlfriend or robbed his neighbour? There must be, nothing else explained this. Jeez!

'Help!' he screamed into the darkness, and a door clanked open. Thank god! Now a sane conversation could start. They would've nabbed the right Rishi Mathur by now, if Rishi Mathur was who they wanted. Bastards! He would read them the riot act, let them know he wasn't taking this lying down like some dumb foreigner. He would sue them for wrongful detention—make them bloody compensate . . .

Two officers walked in. He was right—they'd come to talk to him.

'Do you know Khalid Mohammad Siddiqui?'

That was the first question. And it went on . . . and on . . . for hours . . . days . . . endless . . . Rishi soon lost track of time.

28

Her broken leg up in traction, Zeenat stared at it, seeing not her limb but the olive-green shirt and familiar face. Not in her wildest dreams could she have imagined that the voice she had begun to trust and listen to would be his. Her heart had sought refuge in the accepting space she'd found in him, her bubbling emotions rising up to meet a heart that understood and calmed her. Else, she would've been on the boil endlessly. And yet, to know that Rishi was her saviour was scalding! She squirmed in pain, her leg numb, her mind restless and her heart confused.

Even if it were Shehzad, she would've laughed and swallowed it. He knew every inch of her, it wouldn't have been this awkward if he'd chanced to peer inside her as well. But Rishi! They had always run parallel to one another, never intending to meet, looking straight ahead or the other way. Each took extra pains to avoid the other. What a wallop it had been to learn she had archived all her secrets in him. Life had become a joke—turning slapstick and mean. She shivered at this new reality. And that brought the nurse over.

'Need another painkiller?'

It took some time for Zeenat to switch back to the present, her mind was all topsy-turvy, but now she realized that weights and a pulley were helping keep her left leg in position. Well, the medical world is not so patient or sympathetic. The nurse moved on to other blast victims who were awake and hankered for her professional care and attention.

Zeenat had not seen her come and she didn't see her go. Her mind wandered back to the station, to that most ungainly moment in her life, when she found out that the man she had been thirsting to meet was the one she had always thought dry and dour. Such a tectonic slip was bound to send her mind and emotions haywire. And life had done one worse—it even snatched the ground from under her feet and pitched her right into the middle of a bomb blast, just a second after her seismic encounter. Not a moment did she get to assess the emotional damage.

It wasn't just her heart, even her brain and eyes needed fixing. At least, that was how she saw it. But the doctors were concerned only with her leg and had scheduled her for surgery as soon as one of the OTs freed up. She hadn't been told all that much, not that she cared to know. She wasn't going anywhere for quite some time. There was much to be figured out, and she wasn't good at thinking on her feet. They could keep her in bed for a whole week and she'd be okay with it.

Mullah hurried through the ward, his heart breaking as he passed beds and beds of burnt, wounded and disfigured victims from the blast site. Till he reached his princess. She looked so frail and so inelegant, with her leg sticking up like a scarecrow's hand, all the colour gone from her face and a breath that came heavy and laboured.

'Zeenat, you shouldn't have gone to that museum,' he lamented.

'Museum?' She woke up from her daydream to ask.

'You don't remember? Are you okay . . . is your head fine? Tell me!'

She looked blank and that upped his concern and hysteria. Had she lost her memory? Or was it concussion? Running back to the doctor in charge of the ward, he checked on the exact status of his princess's injuries. Why wasn't she responding adequately? She was in shock, he was told—post-traumatic shock. And they were right in a way. Her heart was in shock and her mind traumatized.

Praying fervently, Mullah begged Allah that his daughter recover enough to lead a normal life with everything and everyone she knew and loved. Love made him think of Ali and he wondered if Ali had got the chance to meet her and profess his love before the bomb had gone off.

'Ali! Did you meet Ali?' he inquired even as they were wheeling her away for surgery.

'Ali?' she repeated, looking lost. Then sighed, 'If only it were Ali . . . things would have been so simple . . .'

Mullah caught on to that one word he wanted to hear. Ali. She remembered him! Also, she sounded like she was keen on him. He rubbed his hands in glee and thanked Allah profusely for granting his wishes with such speed. His mind now raced ahead to start planning for the wedding once she was done with the surgery and the hospital. He would have to be patient, he knew. A bride could not look ravishing hobbling on one leg.

While he fantasized, a crazed media thronged outside. Waiting for a sound bite, a story, a quote, a candid shot, anything at all that would make for an exclusive in the next broadcast or the morning newspaper. They had reported on the seven people killed and the larger number that was injured. Every inch of the blasted Holborn station had been shown again and again. The reaction from Downing Street had been telecast, debated and done away with. Scotland Yard, as usual, had not been very forthcoming; on being hounded for an update, it had let out that forensics were on the job, trying to home in on the type of bomb. And yes, they had picked up suspects, but as of now, there was nothing more to say.

So the air was thick with rumour and conjecture, a lethal mix, way thicker than the smoke from the blast. The injured at the hospital could definitely tell more, as they had been there, and seen what the tight-lipped officers hadn't. Every patient that got discharged was thus waylaid by reporters and cameras, and pestered to rewind to that horrendous moment and cough out every bit they could.

Not much was known except what had already been reported. It had been a single blast, and not a series as had been feared earlier. An unexploded device had been discovered by an alert guard, near the riverfront. It had since been defused by the bomb squad. But even that turned out to be a bomb dating back to the Second World War. Holborn appeared to have been the sole target. It was a small, busy station, the perfect site for a terror attack, promising maximum casualties and footage.

As night crept in, the media got a bite to chew on. The main suspect was an Indian. Not from Iraq. Not from Jordan or Syria. The tabloids and channels went berserk conjecturing who it may be and why.

Indian? Mullah shook his head. No place was free of the menace now. Things would get bleaker for South Asians in London now. He shook his head again as he called up Fiza.

He told her to check on the tenants before she came to see Zeenat. 'Check on Ali first,' he said, 'make sure he's okay. He is more important to us.'

By the time Zeenat came out of surgery, the media had stumbled upon a whole new cult of terrorists to feast upon. Scotland Yard had given them a tasty bite. It would be splashed on the front page of all the papers tomorrow morning. The channels had enough meat for their late-night shows and got busy putting it all together. This new development had something to do with a tattoo. Or at least that's what Mullah had picked up from the hospital grapevine.

29

He heard the cell door open again and shrunk back. He no longer wanted to see them. Once, ages ago, when they first brought him here, he had prayed for some official to come so that they could talk and he could clear his name. All that innocence was now dead and buried in the stale air of this almost windowless, grey, cramped cell.

It was pointless telling them the truth, for they grilled him on things of which he had no clue. They tried to beat it out of him. They got nothing, for he had nothing, and this riled them badly, leading to more insane questions and a more sullen silence on his part. His mind had fallen asleep, and his battered body was now refusing to install a new coping mechanism every day. How long had it been since they brought him here? Days? Months? Years? Time had ceased to matter within these walls. Surviving every interrogation was an achievement in itself, marking a level of endurance he had never known he possessed. Beyond that, life—or the shadow of life he led here—was boring and repetitive.

Two figures staggered in. He heard them come, but he did not rise or look up from his corner, till one addressed him by name.

'Rishi!'

He knew that voice! His head jerked up, eyes dilated, and his breath caught. It was a familiar voice . . . he had stopped hoping for such a miracle.

That was . . . that was . . . Ali! And . . . Shehzad!

Rishi sat gaping, not daring to believe that they were real. He waited for them to come up to him, if they were there in flesh and blood. Devoid of hope and resigned to accept this as another figment of his delirious imagination, he sat still.

'Rishi!' Shehzad shook him by his shoulders and called out his name.

'You okay, mate?' bellowed Ali, drawing near.

Rishi nodded his head, wordless.

After days—maybe months—he was once again overcome with emotion. Life in captivity had reduced him to a zombie in every way, numbing his thoughts and emotions. And then out of the blue, he had company. Rishi wept with joy.

Finally, he had someone to pour it all out to. The way these Brits had screwed him, catching him for being at a station. Thousands of others had been there too. Why him? Then throwing him here, locking him up like they do with a dog, slapping all kinds of charges on him, trying to link him to groups he knew nothing about. They'd cross-examined every bloody thing he'd done these ten years. Hell, even the music he liked was being questioned. Telling them he was only an agony uncle cut no ice. They prodded him to confess stuff he didn't know about . . . had never done. They were making him out to be someone else, someone they could pin the blast on. Bloody racist pigs! Forcing him, torturing his body and playing dirty mind games to kill his spirit. He got bent, but did not break—not yet at least.

'You . . .' he got up and pointed at Ali and Shehzad. 'You go tell the world! Shout my truth out to them! You . . . you know it. Tell them all. Now,' he said, wiping his tears.

Ali hugged him then, squeezing the breath out of his frail frame. Shehzad swore loudly and hit his fist on the wall.

Rishi let go of Ali to stop Shehzad. 'Don't. They're watching us. Don't upset them. They won't let you come again.'

Shehzad laughed then. But this was not his laugh . . . not at all. Something was not right. He looked at Ali.

The Pakistani's eyes had misted. 'Janaab . . . we're all screwed.'

Rishi's world spun again. He lurched on to the wall for support, and waited for his head to stop spinning. The numbness was coming back too. Shehzad and Ali rushed forward to catch him, unnerved by his state. They had been through hell too. But Rishi probably faced the brunt of it as he was the one at Holborn, and they, in the vicinity. Bloody Asians! Bloody terrorists! That's how England was now branding them—ever since that blasted evening.

In some time, Rishi got a grip of himself, stood up straight and gave them a twisted smile. Their faces seemed consumed with concern. He peered closer, seeing them properly for the first time since they had entered his cell. His housemates didn't look very good. In fact, they . . . they looked like him. Like zombies. For, they were prisoners too, caught like him, screwed by fate and the colour of their skin. All three of them were paying for having been at the wrong place at the wrong time.

'Why?' It took a while for Rishi to scrape out that one word. Why had they picked on his housemates?

'It's easier to believe outsiders are the wrong ones. Happens all the time.'

That was Ali. Rishi saw the Pakistani's frame shudder in disgust. He was boiling inside, but there was nothing he could do about it.

'Why the hell did you go to Holborn, Rishi?' Shehzad vented it out on the Indian. He had to do it to someone, else he would go mad.

Rishi understood his state—he felt the same way.

'Zeenat.'

'Zeenat?'

Ali and Shehzad cried out in one voice, not understanding why Rishi, of all people, would have gone anywhere for her. The two couldn't stand each other.

Rishi eyed her two suitors warily. Two pairs of eyes pierced through him, sharp and incisive, questioning him. He couldn't meet them today. Hell! Where to start and how? His mind was stuttering. They'd been through so much already and were hurting badly. This would bleed them more. How could he do it to them?

Ali shook him hard. 'Out with it, mate.'

'Shehzad,' began Rishi, sweating, 'you remember that girl I was chatting with?'

Shehzad looked blank.

'Go on,' Ali was squirming in impatience.

'That night you came to my room and found me online? That . . . that . . .'

Shehzad's eyes widened in shock. 'That was Zeenie?' He couldn't swallow this. Why, she was staying over with them that night. On the sofa, at their place. And all that time, this crap was going on? Girls! He should've known. They're all one colour and creed—sick!

Rishi saw the Bangla face go white, and it pained him to see his friend this way. He knew the baggage the fellow carried . . . this could pull him under. Rishi had never wanted it to be this way. He hadn't known it was Zeenat, nor had he known this guy was so serious about her.

'Shehzad, I didn't know it was her.' Desperately, he tried to reach out to him. But Shehzad looked lost. 'I . . . I saw her there, first time that day.'

'What?' Ali found his voice and asked, 'She was at Holborn too?'

Rishi nodded, unable to look up or speak.

'Have they got her too?' Ali shot back.

'I don't know.'

The three of them looked at each other. This had not struck them before. Mired in their own shit, it had not entered their heads that she might also be drowning in the same mess.

'We didn't meet,' Rishi told them. 'We couldn't . . . the bomb went off.' In their eyes, he saw the same dread that had overtaken him at the station when he couldn't find her.

'You're one shady fellow,' Ali declared, finding it tough to digest this news.

'He said he didn't know,' Shehzad bounced back, seeing Rishi go to pieces. 'Don't kill a dead man.'

Before Ali could hit back, Rishi took control of the conversation. 'No one's dead. And no one's going to be either.'

'I won't let anyone mess with me!' Ali was still aggravated.

'We're in this together,' Rishi looked the Pakistani in the eye as he spoke.

Shehzad was getting the drift, and tried to calm down his housemate. 'Our battle's with them,' he reminded Ali, pointing at the door. 'Not with each other.'

'You're right,' agreed the Pakistani and held out his hand to both.

Their countries, their love, their suffering—all of it ceased to matter. The three of them came together as one again that day in that cell. They stood holding hands, like Zeenat would make them do, in a promise of friendship and support. Forever.

'Wait,' Shehzad cried out as they were about to let go of each other. His eye fell on the tattoo he'd etched on each of their wrists. 'They kept grilling me about this tattoo.'

'Me too,' boomed Ali the very next second.

Rishi nodded a yes as the other two turned to him for confirmation. So it was the damn tattoo that had further messed things up. That tiny bowl of curry on their three wrists, it clubbed them together—and alarmed the British agencies no end.

'Shehzad!' Rishi and Ali were both at his neck. This Bangla dude spelt trouble even when he tried to do good.

'Relax,' Shehzad shook the boys off. 'Stop attacking like the fucking Brits.'

It was left to Rishi once again to restore order. As they sat cramped together, debating their next step, Rishi made a suggestion. 'Let's first get all our stories out—leaving nothing out.'

'Yes,' seconded Ali. 'We need to stitch up the bits.'

'You start,' Shehzad said to Rishi.

The Indian began, recounting to them his days as an agony uncle, the flood of mails he handled and how. His mates nodded in complete understanding—that sounded exactly like the Rishi they knew. He came to her letters next, recalling how they grabbed his attention and then his heart. A girl losing her world overnight and crying out for help.

'So Mullah was not her father,' observed Shehzad, relating to her shock completely. He had felt the same way when his family crumbled.

'We got chatting, and one thing led to another . . . and we decided to meet.'

'Only you didn't,' said Ali, barging in to clarify that one important point.

Rishi said nothing.

Shehzad put an arm around Rishi's shoulders—the fellow had really been hit hard. He could see it in the Indian's eyes, in the things he didn't say. Damn love—it messed you real bad.

Rishi filled them in on his arrest. How he hadn't known that he was being arrested until much later when he woke up. He told them about the cross-questioning, the confinement, the muck they gave him . . . and were still giving. He left nothing out.

Ali began with Mullah's offer. Eyebrows raised, his mates heard him out, including his confession of love.

'So, that's the story of your paper lion,' Shehzad butted in.

Ali let that pass and revealed how he'd followed Shehzad to the museum on foot.

The Bangladeshi picked up the tale from there. Zeenat had herself told him she would be at the museum.

'What?' Rishi found this difficult to believe.

No, she wasn't meeting him there, the Bangladeshi clarified. Probably, it was just an excuse to fob him off. Running into the Pakistani there had been a major shock. Each had painted the other a villain, till news of the explosion filtered through. And they ran to Holborn station, knowing this was where Rishi had gone.

When a cop on the way asked them to slow down, Ali lost his cool. Told him to let them go in the name of Allah to save his friend. That made the cop more suspicious, and he stopped the Pakistani altogether. Shehzad tried to explain, but that didn't get them anywhere. The cop ordered the Bangladeshi to get into the car as well.

'And since that day, we've been in jail, answering questions.'

Ali picked up from where Shehzad left off. 'They want to know about our families, friends, our enemies—even if we don't have one, still they want to know about it. And this tattoo! They can't stop harping on it.'

The Pakistani paused to catch his breath. 'I told them it was a bowl of my curry. They said they're no fools!'

'But that's bloody well what they are,' Rishi screamed, banging his fist on the toilet seat that occupied the corner.

'Exactly,' agreed Shehzad, holding his friend back lest he injure himself. 'Their stupidity is what got us in this . . . and that maybe can get us out too one day. I don't exactly know how though,' he told the two sets of eyes latching on to him intently now. 'But somewhere, it will show up. Let's just stand together. They got nothing on us. And there is nothing. So . . .'

That made sense, and they had nothing else to look up to either. So on Shehzad's sage advice, they ended that day.

30

The media had been feasting on the tattoo relentlessly, since the day of the blast. After the Indian, the authorities had zeroed in on to two more terror suspects, based on the CCTV footage of the area. Even these turned out to be Asians, all sporting the same tattoo. A question was being asked again and again—were Asians becoming a threat to Great Britain?

As for the tattoo, all kinds of stories were afloat. Some called it the circle of terror. Others took it to be a cup of non-Muslim blood. And there were those who saw it as a pit for the infidels. The speculation factory was working overtime, feeding on mass hysteria, what with Scotland Yard warning of more such attacks.

Zeenat threw aside the newspaper and cursed the British in such colourful language that her mother would surely have had a cardiac arrest, and Shehzad, he would have been proud of her. Hobbling up to her bedroom door, she screamed out for Mullah. He wrapped up his prayer and rushed to his baby, hoping she was okay.

'See! See what filth they're printing.' And she pointed her crutch at the pages of the paper littering the floor of her room.

Mullah obediently picked up the pages, put them together and read the parts she was frothing about. He cursed too, not audibly though. The boys were in big trouble. By Allah's grace, he was married to a British lady, else they would also have been under the scanner. The stories he'd been hearing at the mosque were disquieting. To the white people, every Asian was a terrorist now.

'Zeenat, you rest. Don't worry about all this. Inshallah, all will be well soon.'

Zeenat was livid. 'Am I a two-year-old?' she asked him, her eyes dancing with fury. 'Or you think I'm brain dead?' As she was regaining her strength, her drama was returning too.

Mullah smiled indulgently. His fiery girl was back.

'I don't understand you! While your countrymen are being crucified, you stand there smiling, posing like some Mona Lisa.' With that, she fell back on the pillows and covered her face with the bed sheet.

Giving her a whole minute to indulge in her dramatics, Mullah ambled up to her bed and stroked her head. 'What do you want me to do?'

'Get them out of jail,' she ordered, throwing off the sheet in a trice to look him in the eye.

'I can't. You know that. This is not India or Pakistan—the authorities won't listen to me.'

'If it were me, would you give up like this?'

Mullah had no answer to this. She had trapped him yet again.

'C'mon. Tell me!' She wasn't one to let go so fast.

'It's not that I don't want to,' he tried to explain, 'I can't.'

'You can't, but you surely know someone who can.'

She was bright. Mullah knew when he was beaten. His chest though puffed up in pride, thinking how well he had brought her up. She was a class act—strong, smart and incurably theatrical. An Oscar mix!

'Let me see . . . let me see what I can do. I know this lobbying firm—let me talk to them.'

Zeenat gave him a kiss; that always worked fast with him. She knew him well.

Mullah was putty in her hands now. He stroked her head one last time before going on his errand. 'You're worried for Ali, no? Don't be. I'll take care of it.' And he left, not seeing her frown at his parting shot.

Ali? Why did Mullah think this was about Ali? Whatever, she reasoned, as long as he was on the job, that was all that mattered.

Not an hour had gone by when the house was shaken again. Not by Zeenat this time. It was the police. They had called on the landline and asked for Mullah. Fiza took the call and in a poised tone let them know he was out on business and she was in charge.

The cops wanted to search house number 104 on George Street and Mohammed Mullah was listed as the owner of the property. She requested them to wait, but got a curt response that they would be raiding the premises any time now. Mullah should therefore report to the station immediately and cooperate with the search.

Not showing the panic she felt, Fiza called Mullah and said, 'Drop whatever you're doing and come home right now.' Her voice was even, but he perceived the undercurrent of tension and fear. Cancelling his appointment with the lobbyist company, he rushed home to his begum. Soon, to his daughter's utter irritation, the couple got busy trying to save the family name and house, forgetting the boys' case.

A distinguished citizen of the island country, Mullah was asked to not hold back any point he felt he should report in the name of national security. 'If only they could've kept his house tidier . . .' was the one grouse he aired to the cops. While being questioned, Mullah revealed zilch, but raiding the house threw up many surprises. Shehzad's room was full of tattoo designs, inks, posters, knick-knacks and a drawer full of antidepressants. The search team also found a compass box wrapped in red cloth and slipped into a zip pouch beneath his shirts.

Ali seemed to have stored every kind of spice in the world in his room. There was enough masala in there to flavour the whole damn universe. In his cupboard they came across a number of diaries and notebooks with Urdu writings. These were of special interest to the investigators, and experts were called in to translate the notes. The flared interest deflated fast when the writing turned out to be only recipes and poetry. Rishi's room was barren, save for some clothes and paper and greeting cards. His laptop, however, was overflowing with mail. The officer scrutinizing it scratched his head not knowing what to make of all this agony uncle crap infesting the Indian's inbox.

Where the cops go, the media cannot be far behind. They flounced in, taking as close a peek as they could get, and managed to shoot the stuff the investigating officers had dug up for forensics. Besides two laptops, stacks of books and diaries, a pressure cooker and a compass box had been seized. At least, that's what the press got to see and report.

This house number 104, on George Street, is where the suspected bomber trio stayed holed up. What were the Asians plotting and preparing here? And what of that cavernous kitchen device the investigators have stumbled upon? Was that a pressure-cooker bomb in the making? Only time and investigations will tell.

A beautiful compass meanwhile was found in the Bangladeshi's room. A dated beauty, its point was once used for etching. What does this say about them—that even their art is violent?

The reporters and anchors were having a field day leveraging the raid scene to grab eyeballs. Senior officers at the police headquarters said they were collecting intelligence from all three countries of the suspects to build a dossier of evidence.

Fiza switched off the TV. Seeing their house flashed across international television and watching this whole thing unfold was becoming a nightmare. The boys were totally done in. The one twinge she felt was for Ali. Well, there would be other boys for Zeenat. If need be, she could always import one from Karachi.

Zeenat jumped around on her one good leg, overtaken in equal measure by anger and anxiety. Footage of house number 104 had invoked so many happy memories that she felt like crying. But the sensational coverage also had her recoiling in disgust.

'God! They are even playing up Shehzad's compass,' she exclaimed, seething in rage. 'That's crass invasion of the boys' privacy.' She was getting increasingly jittery about the wild media conjectures and the nasty statements the police were making.

Mullah returned just that instant from the police station. He looked drained, as the cops had tried to squeeze out every possible detail from the landlord of the terror suspects.

Zeenat believed her wonder father could upturn every seemingly impossible situation. But even she did not have the heart to demand anything from him right then.

She didn't need to. Mullah saw it in her eyes and her muteness. His alert eyes took in the fidget spinner her fingers toyed with as she stared blankly out of the living room window.

Refusing the tea Fiza had just brought, he dialled the lobbying company to reschedule his appointment. Things had struck closer home now and he would need to act fast. This firm could buy access to every department in the government and was known to wield considerable influence with the powers that be. Such relationships are forged over years, on a bedrock of trust and favour, and Mullah had great respect for them. But first he needed to get his house and family neatly separated from this mess. Then he would take up the case of Ali and the other two boys, and see if they could be released.

Zeenat's faith in Mullah had not been unfounded. Hearing him talk on the phone told her it was just a matter of time before things would be fine again.

Putting the phone down, Mullah picked up the remote to catch a bite of the news before he left for the appointment.

'*As we report, a car with four unexploded bombs has been seized in Manchester. The driver was shot dead while trying to escape. Reports of there being one more person in the car are doing the rounds, but the police are not confirming anything.*

'*Yes, the bombs could be the same as the one used at Holborn. The identity of the driver is yet to be given out. He was carrying no papers on him. The body has now been sent for postmortem. That was the Manchester Police making a statement to the media. Questions on there being a second person in the car were fobbed off.*

'"*For operational reasons, we cannot share any more information with you right now.*"

'Simply locking up the three Asians, it seems, has failed to secure Britain. Have the investigations revealed anything substantial to fend off more disasters? What's the next step? That's a question the government and the police need to answer very soon.'

Mullah closed his eyes and tried to make sense of what this latest development meant for him and his family, especially Zeenat. Ten minutes later, he was out of the house, taking a walk. He had decided to bunk the lobbyist appointment and instead meet with the Labour MP he knew. This was an emergency and he couldn't rely on anyone but himself. All this breaking news was threatening to break him.

31

Inside the cell, Ali tossed from left to right, trying to catch a wink or two. But there was too much clogging his mind, not allowing him to rest. So he had been right! That vile Bangladeshi had been eyeing his would-be begum on the sly. The scum even had the gall to steal his kebab and then use it to steal his girl. There was no way he could forgive him. Never! But more than this, what was messing his heart was Zeenat's tryst with Rishi. He just couldn't understand it. She hated talking to Rishi upfront. Or even talking about him. Yet she loved chatting with him online. How could that be? And that Bangladeshi Romeo! He eyed every moving skirt. How could he possibly fall in love with just one girl? That too the one who was to be his begum?

This was messy. He could lose this match. That would mean no begum, no Mullah, and no hotel. Ali sighed. But he did have Rishi . . . and that Shehzad too. The one thing his heart knew for sure now was that these two would always be with him, come what may. That now helped him sleep soundly for the first time in a long time.

Rishi lay awake, thinking. Shehzad's museum story haunted him. His plastic-heart proposal had not happened, but the depth of this boy's feelings jolted him. Had he intruded wrongly? Not that he had intended to. Even he had planned a proposal, though nothing so dashing as Shehzad—just a short piece he'd rehearsed to deliver at the London Eye. When the capsule of the Ferris wheel was high up there, and the city floated down below, with the Thames flowing beneath majestically, he'd say his piece. Wasn't something novel, he had seen many tourists do it before. But they hadn't done it with his girl—so it would be new for her. That had been his cheesy logic. But even that moment was lost to him now.

Ali snored. And Rishi recalled his lion tattoo. The Pakistani's act had plastered him completely. He knew the guy was besotted with her, but going to such lengths? He'd never thought the bugger had the crazy lover gene in him. Shit! Zeenat had invaded all three hearts. Did she even know what she had done?

The stars had faded outside. It was time for sunlight. But in Rishi's head, it was still dark because he had no answers.

Shehzad was the first to wake up. This was another seismic shift of sorts. The prison cell had probably realigned his inner cells. But getting up early in a prison is a sheer waste as there is nothing to do. Except to think. And curse. Or pray, which again may be looked upon with suspicion if you happen to be Muslim. The Bangladeshi looked at his two housemates, now cellmates too, their faces tense, even in sleep. No, they weren't having any happy dreams like before. Life had changed. And so had their perceptions, be they awake or asleep.

How naïve they had been, Shehzad lay thinking. Talking of reuniting countries, the subcontinent—the world. What dreamers they had been! But this world . . . this world was bloody different. It thought differently. Racist mindsets and extremist thinking don't change. 'Bloody Asians!' they'd said. A shudder went through him. His blood boiled every time he heard or thought of this. Yet he had lived with it. And how these colour-crazed jerks had screwed him and his mates. He shivered again.

'Shehzad?' asked Rishi. 'What's wrong?'

'Everything. Everything is wrong.' All of Shehzad's frustration slipped out in that one statement.

Rishi turned to face him fully. There was barely space, squashed as the three were in that hellish hole.

'Together we can . . .'

Shehzad cut Rishi and his calming talk. 'Together? Together doesn't exist in this fucking world. Everyone's out to screw someone.'

Ali had got up by now and was listening in, completely in tune with what the Bangladeshi boy felt.

Rishi knew the Bangladeshi was right in a way. Hell, he didn't even get a family that stayed together. Rishi cursed himself for preaching.

'All that bullshit we were dreaming back then . . .' continued Shehzad, 'Bangla–Pak–India together . . . it was stupid . . . we were such fools . . . complete idiots.'

Ali looked at Shehzad and asked, 'Are you upset with me, Shehzad?'

'This is not about you . . . not us . . . no.'

Rishi spoke up then. 'I get what you're trying to say. You're right—we're okay with each other, but that's it. Going beyond it is madness. The world won't turn our way.'

'Exactly.'

Ali was not liking this talk. He still believed in a world where people came together after drifting apart.

'Borders won't go,' Rishi pronounced.

'And they shouldn't,' asserted his Bangladeshi housemate.

'Days, months . . . whatever I have spent here, I've grown up,' replied the Indian. 'Now, I realize it. People won't buy it. Peace and harmony is one thing. Ideology completely another.'

'Xenophobia rules,' rued Ali.

'Ali, don't you follow?' Shehzad drove in. 'Even if you hypnotize the masses, your governments will snap you out of it. Power and paisa are all they want. Nothing else.'

'And even if we get it, we can't manage it,' pointed out Rishi. 'China's shitting us already in Ladakh. And Arunachal. No way can we control that long Afghan border.'

'Afghanistan's one big headache,' admitted Ali.

'Took us years to get rid of Khalistan. This would be like . . . we're importing Balochistan. And Waziristan. Why should we?'

'You got enough Naxals and their Naga–Mizo cousins to keep you busy,' Shehzad added with a snigger.

'Yes, makes no sense,' agreed Rishi. 'We couldn't catch one Dawood. Taliban and al-Qaeda will together drive us nuts.'

'I still think we'll become big if we team up,' insisted Ali, not ready to fully abandon the idea of reunifying. 'These Brits and Americans will come licking our asses then.'

'You seriously think so? Grow up, fool!' Shehzad said, brushing aside the Pakistani's rose-tinted view.

'The world won't let it happen, Ali,' Rishi put it in black and white to his mate.

Ali looked unconvinced.

'You think China will want to lose you? No way. Even the Arabs won't want to see you go with India.'

'Why?'

'Because you're this big Islamist nation. And you got this huge army, air force . . . plus nuclear weapons.'

'And . . .' pitched in Shehzad, 'even the US won't let you out of their clutches . . . cause there goes boom their biggest arms market.'

'Why are you singing a new tune today?' Ali was not getting it. 'Earlier, you were all for it.'

'That was yesterday,' Rishi's voice had a chill. 'See where we're today. Locked up.'

'Don't you still get it, Ali?' Shehzad was getting impatient and irritated. 'It's the mentality—you can't wipe it away. The West was racist, is, and will stay that way. We'll only fuck up what we have now by trying to unite. That will only divide us more.'

'Maybe you're right,' Ali's voice was low.

'We could do an EU kind of thing,' Rishi proposed tentatively. 'Build on SAARC. But even that might not work.' His voice had lost all the optimism of before. The ways of humans had wrecked every hope he had dared to nurture.

'South Asians forming a joint armed forces,' jeered Shehzad, 'that's stuff for science fiction!'

'Right. Trade and currency maybe. But not other things.' Rishi was with Shehzad on this.

'Independence is what people want. Not unity,' declared Shehzad.

'You, Bangla baby, you shut up,' attacked Ali. 'Most of your country gets flooded every damn year. Whoever survives then tries to sneak over to India . . . and you . . . you talk of independence!'

'But Ali, even India won't really want Bangladesh to join us. We do stand with them,' explained Rishi. 'But all these terror factories opening up everywhere, we're scared.'

'So we end up with what we started—trade, commerce, tourism and culture,' Ali listed in a flat tone.

'Well, we can try and stop fighting. And build more confidence.'

'Aw, shut up, you two! You're sounding bloody like the Foreign Office.'

Shehzad was done with all this subcontinental shit. All he wanted now was food, not that he was going to get some any time soon. But this shit? It had to stop—right away.

'We talk and we rot. Nothing more is left in our lives now.'

No one challenged this statement. The bleak and miserable tone in which Ali stated this was proof enough. But life has a way of changing suddenly, and going exactly the way you never expected it to go.

By the end of next week, all three were out again in the open. Released on police bail, with no conditions attached.

32

Zeenat picked up the evening newspaper. Ever since the terror incident, the media had been in a frenzy, running series after series of highly speculative stories about the blast suspects. They had been carrying opinion pieces that condemned their act, and now upped the ante to control immigration from Asian nations. Also, there was a lot of general terror-bashing in its pages. All of this was guaranteed to wreck her mood. Still, she could not stop reading it. For now, this was her only connection with her friends.

Fiza stood at the door and saw her daughter's face change as she began to read:

'The Holborn blast detainees have been released on pre-charge bail. The police will continue to investigate the case, but said it was no longer necessary to keep the three locked up in the high-security prison. Does that mean the trio no longer pose a risk to the country and our people? Or is this a case of police nerves, as they cannot detain them much longer? Pre-charge suspects can be held for a maximum of fourteen days under the amended PACE law. And they had been in jail just one day short of two weeks. Is the amended law helping them escape? What guarantee is there that this will not become another Khalid story, the terror suspect who left for Syria whilst on bail?

'It's been almost a fortnight since the blasts, but there are more questions than answers. Why are the security services so wary of making categorical statements? Even Downing Street is reluctant to confirm that the Indian caught at Holborn Tube station was the main bomber. Labour MP Jim Gilbert, however, has been intensely lobbying for their release. He told BBC Radio, "Even if the authorities assumed they were linked to the blast and arrested them, you cannot keep someone locked up forever only on suspicion."

'The lawyer MP has not shied from casting aspersions on the police force. "No doubt there is someone in the security services who wants to delay their release simply because it suits their individual purposes." The ruling party has condemned the statement as irresponsible. However, human rights groups like Amnesty International, Liberty and Redress are gathering around the Labour MP, pressurizing the government to release the suspects unless specific charges justify their detention. They are demanding that the government immediately come out with a full report on the arrests and subsequent investigations.

'The tattoo mystery is also yet to be solved. Sources reveal that the new suspect picked up during the Manchester bomb haul has led to many more arrests. The police are tight-lipped on this development. A new Daesh group, Fatah-al-Islamiya has claimed responsibility for both the Holborn blast

as well as the Manchester bomb haul. A video going viral
for the same is being verified by agencies. If the video proves
authentic, the Holborn blast suspects could escape trial.'

Zeenat sprang up from her chair and whooped with joy, squealing in pain the next second, for her operated leg was not used to such sudden movements. Fiza ran in to help her get back to her seat. But Zeenat wanted to be driven over to the boys' place. Before Fiza could object, Zeenat had changed her mind—she decided to wait. She needed to plan out the whole meeting in her head first. Not that she had not imagined it in her head many times already, but that had been a colourful Bollywood version full of *naach-gaana* and mushy dialogue. This would be for real. All of a sudden, she felt awkward and shy to meet the boys—the same boys with whom she had always been so comfortable. The next hour or two, she kept flitting between going and not going.

Thankfully, she was spared the decision. The boys came over. They were at her door. Was it like the movies, where the heart can sense the arrival of loved ones before your eyes and ears see or hear them? Actually, no. No one, absolutely no one, rang the bell at their house at this hour of the evening. Mullah would return only an hour later, so logic claimed it had to be them. A part of Zeenat wanted to believe it was like the movies. It refused to accept any other reason, and made her scurry to get ready for the meetup.

Meanwhile, Fiza was greeting and ushering them in. The trio looked worn-out, but at peace. They wanted to meet Mullah.

'He won't be back for another hour,' she replied.

All three got up at once to leave, saying they would be back when he returned.

'Have some coffee? Or stay for dinner.'

Thanking her for her kindness, they made to go.

'How dare you!' That stopped them in their tracks. 'You bastards! I get you out, and it's Mullah you want to meet?' Hobbling out into the hall, Zeenat was clearly breathing hellfire.

All three did a U-turn and stood gawking. At their love. Standing up there on one good foot. Her voice and spirit as high as ever. Her eyes dancing with rage, nostrils flared and cheeks turning redder by the minute. It warmed their hearts. Seeing her angry and feisty had been too much to hope for. Yet, god had granted them this valley of joy amidst their mountains of misfortune. They smiled at this unexpected gift.

She tottered up closer. 'I'm mad at you, and you idiots are grinning? Have you lost it?'

Pointing to her hurt foot, Shehzad inquired, 'Who you been dancing with?'

She slapped him. All that nervous tension, the pain of waiting and not knowing, and her flip-flop of moods and emotions had taken their toll. It all spurted out in that one extreme reaction, the only reply she was capable of. All three rushed to hold her as she burst out, for she had lost her balance and was about to fall. It was a comic scene. Fiza left them at that. These over-the-top, sentimental displays had never been her cup of tea.

They hung around, swapping stories. The boys regaled her with prison tales. Zeenat enacted how the hysterical media had ballooned up their curry tattoo to cult status. It was back to old times, with Ali and Shehzad vying for her attention, quibbling over every little thing, while Rishi hemmed and hawed and spoke as little as before.

Mullah returned, but only to cloud their happy picnic. 'A police bail is just that,' he pointed out. 'Not a release or pardon. Any time,' he said with a snap of his fingers, 'they can cancel it any time. And pick you up again.'

'That's not what I asked for,' Zeenat accosted him. 'Why are you doling me half measures? I want it all cleared!'

Mullah was at a loss. His daughter was a monster when it came to having her own way, but this time he could not give her what she wanted. 'Zeenat,' he started, looking fondly at his daughter, 'I'm trying, my dear . . . I'm trying.'

The boys took leave, Ali finding it difficult to not choke at the way Zeenat had just tamed the roaring bully of a Mullah, ticking him off even when he was sweating it out to gift her the impossible. He'd been lobbying in the hallowed halls of power with god only knew whatnot. Shehzad relaxed. His freedom was now not his problem. It was Mullah's problem. He winked at her in appreciation. Rishi, however, was avoiding this goodbye routine. He had slipped safely into his earlier role of a wallflower till she sent things again for a six at the door, with just two words: 'Take care.'

Rishi's whole world turned upside down once again.

33

'The CCTVs misled us,' admitted the police, buckling under the media glare and pressure from human rights groups. The supposedly suspect activity of the South Asians that these cameras recorded that day were found to be only as dubious as that of any other lover in London on Valentine's Day. Further interrogation and monitoring of the suspects had ruled out their involvement beyond reasonable doubt. The house search and other investigations had led to nothing substantial against the Indian or the Bangladeshi. There was no case to be made out against the English-speaking Pakistani chef either, except maybe the possible charge of possessing a pressure cooker, a potentially explosive device.

The new suspect in the police net had taken the investigation on to a totally different track and country, leading to further significant arrests and discoveries, including a new terrorist network. So the old suspects had to be released, and for good this time. But a month got eaten up—two weeks inside jail and two outside—before this clean chit came about.

Mullah's friend in the Labour Party had all along ranted against the gross injustice meted out to the three young immigrants. He raised significant questions, pulling up the authorities for unnecessarily extending pre-charge detention with police bail, when they had no evidence to look for, as the investigation was going nowhere. 'Should you justify holding on to suspects while you request for "more time" in the hope of coming up with something some day?'

The clean chit they got completely clean-bowled Ali and Shehzad and Rishi. After all that bizarre questioning and endless micro-examining of every shade of their lives, none of the three believed they would ever be completely off the hook.

Even Mullah had not expected to reap such large dividends so fast. He owed the Labour Party big time now for having set the wheel of justice into motion. Fiza now expected Mullah's supreme effort to fetch even bigger dividends at home. Zeenat, however, took his role casually in her stride. The boys were innocent and getting them off the racist clutches of the authorities was the sacred duty of every South Asian in this foreign land.

'Foreign? We are British!' Fiza was quick to remind her.

'You may forget your origins, not me.' Zeenat was getting sassier each passing day and Mullah wondered how far she could go before it became too much for his wife.

Ten houses ahead, Rishi too sat wondering about Mullah's daughter. His train of thought was way different from that of the old man. So lost was he in his meanderings that he chewed on Ali's paratha mechanically, forgetting to eat the accompanying alu–gobi. Shehzad slunk up to the plate, substituted the vegetable with some lettuce and stood in the corner to watch the show. Rishi crunched on the lettuce leaves once the paratha got over, not seeing or feeling the taste of anything.

Ali shook his head and, leaving the two fools to their jokes, headed out to his restaurant. Too much time had been lost in jail. He couldn't afford to neglect his work for one more minute now. Even if he slogged every single day and contracted his shoestring expenses to wafer-thinness, he would still need to work for at least 365 more days to earn enough to return home a victor.

An hour and a half later though, he had retreated back to square one. When it came to Nawab Balti, the clean chit from the police was not enough to whitewash Ali's terror taint. A fellow South Asian—a Bangladeshi to be precise—the restaurant owner threw up his hands and shut the door on his favourite chef. Ali's misadventure, he proclaimed in a knowing voice, even if it had been inadvertent, was definitely not good for business. 'I have a respectable place up here. Can't afford any of this bad publicity.' Ali stood dazed, his mind rejecting what his ears were hearing.

Out of a job, Ali walked past the service door to take one last look at the kitchen where he had whipped up not just dishes on the menu, but also his passion for perfection. Wanting to serve a dream every time, and hoping this would one day take him to his own dream. Reality cut into nostalgia with a sharp knife. A substitute chef, with no bombing history or stain, had already been hired. He was busy stirring the onion–tomato gravy. However, Ali did not take it to heart. That period of confinement had freed his mind of many fears and shackles. He now took each moment as it came. Leaning against the wall of another eatery, he did a quick stock-taking. No job meant no work permit, which, in turn, meant no more income or the right to stay in London.

So he bought a ticket on the hop-on–hop-off double-decker bus that took you around the city, stopping at every place earmarked important for the tourist. As he would be leaving the city soon and had nothing to do right now, he might as well see the sights before he left. That night, Ali made the biryani exactly the way Rishi enjoyed it, and also Shehzad's favourite mutton curry. He planned to invite Zeenat too, but she evidently needed no invitation, because he found her at the door when he returned home.

Once the four had their fill, the Pakistani told them about being sacked. 'The taint's not gone yet. The spot has spread far enough to kill my job.'

'What!'

Rishi had thought he had turned shockproof after the two jolts he had got on that one Holborn day last month. Yet Ali's revelation whacked his mind completely. Shehzad lost his voice. And Zeenat her cool. She would have hobbled off to kill that bloody nawab of Nawab Balti if Ali had not held her back by sheer brute force.

They sat staring at each other, finding it difficult to digest this stinker. Hours slid by. Every idea under the sun, moon, stars and man-made satellites was dribbled in that house that night. But there was no going around the work-permit rule. Even if Ali managed to wangle a new job, the chances of him getting another permit were remote in the current anti-immigrant climate storming the British minds.

What was worse, along with the job, his dream too had been sacked. 'And it's not just my dream. It's my ammi's dream. My abbu's dream. And the dream of so many more out there in Lahore.' He said this laughing, but they knew he was crying inside. In fact, they were all weeping inside.

Rishi and Shehzad were ready to pool their resources if that could do the trick. But their wallets refused to cooperate, filled as they were mostly with air.

Suddenly, Zeenat jumped up in excitement, squealing in pain the next second. Excitement made her forget that she had one leg that was not as strong as the other one yet. 'I got the perfect idea. It can get you your dhaba cent per cent!' Her eyes danced as she declared this.

The three boys wondered what was cooking in that unpredictable head of hers.

Seeing them askance, Zeenat challenged them. 'You think I can't, right?'

The three dared not agree, though that's exactly what they thought.

'Okay. I can't. But Mullah . . . Mullah definitely can.'

This was vague. Why the hell would Mullah fund Ali's dhaba. Unless . . . Three pairs of eyes flew to her face. Two in panic, one in wonder. Did she know of Mullah's offer to Ali? Was she actually thinking . . . could she . . . no! It was too outlandish for Rishi and Shehzad to even consider for another second. As for Ali, his heart was beating at ten times its normal pace.

The drama queen took her time to relieve them of their misery. For two whole minutes, the three stayed on edge before she chose to unfurl her sure-shot plan.

'Ali,' she began, 'Mullah, for some weird reason, likes you a lot.' She then paused. The antennas of all three went up. 'He wants to marry me off to you.' Zeenat had no idea what she was doing to them as she took her time in elaborating her great plan. 'Let's exploit that,' she proposed to the Pakistani.

His heart stopped. He would be getting his begum after all. Ali felt like he'd been thrown down from a hundred feet, and was finally entering heaven. 'Jannat,' he mumbled.

Shehzad and Rishi felt only the first part; their heads were hitting ground zero hard.

'Yes, jannat. We'll make Mullah give you your jannat. In pounds.' Zeenat was on her own spin.

The boys were not in a state to make out what more she had to say. Their hearts and minds were malfunctioning.

'Once he funds your dhaba and you fly out, I'll tell him I have changed my mind.'

That was a whopper.

'Meaning?' Ali was almost scared to ask this.

'Meaning . . . I'll call off the phony engagement.'

An earthquake couldn't have shaken the room like she did. The three boys were shell-shocked by her crazy game plan. Only Zeenat could have dreamt up such a whacker, and only she had the gall to carry it off.

Shehzad whistled and picked her up, her injured leg et al, hoisting her high up in his arms like a prize trophy. Rishi pulled a reluctant Ali to his feet and they danced around her in a circle, singing lusty numbers.

Ali was not so sure about this. He did not like deceiving Mullah. 'I'll ask him for a loan instead. We don't need to lie . . .'

Zeenat cut in. 'You don't know him. I do. Only I can wangle the pounds off him.'

Shehzad seconded, 'He won't give you a penny, man.'

Ali was still not okay with it. 'I won't be able to live with it. No.'

Zeenat leaned forward and shook him hard. 'Don't act up. I'm the *dramebaaz* here, not you.'

The Indian and the Bangladeshi clapped.

'And don't you dare refuse a fake engagement with me,' she warned the Pakistani in a hard voice, pointing a finger at him. 'No one, absolutely no one, rejects me.'

Ali gaped at her. He had no answer to this.

'Get it?' She was relentless.

'Got it.'

'What a *paisa vasool* show, Zeenie!' The Bangladeshi saluted his heroine and then ran in to fetch a bottle. He wanted to toast the impending engagement of Ali and Zeenat.

The party had restarted at house number 104, George Street. If only Mullah knew what the morning would bring him.

34

The drive back from the airport was empty and long. Shehzad, Rishi and Zeenat stared out of their windows blankly, rewinding to each other the happy times they had shared with the Pakistani.

Airborne, Ali was doing the same. Looking fixedly at the clouds, he wondered how someone could love him and yet not love him. Zeenat had executed her plan effortlessly. Getting Mullah to cough up the dough had been child's play for her. 'You can't send me off with a pauper,' she had whimpered.

'But why Lahore? I'll set up his restaurant here—in London!' Mullah failed to see the logic of setting up a dhaba in Lahore when the lovebirds would live in his city.

'He's got to see to his family too,' Zeenat explained with the patience one displays with a child who is slow. 'You wouldn't like me abandoning you completely, would you?' She had fired her deadliest missile.

He hadn't argued further. He promptly calculated the amount his future son-in-law would need, and transferred it to the Pakistani's account. The one thing he failed to understand was the boy's need to fly to Lahore.

'Why?'

'Because he's got to meet his family once,' Zeenat adopted the same placid tone with him again.

'What if he gets no visa to return?'

'Surely they won't stop your son-in-law?' Zeenat sounded offended now.

Mullah kept quiet. And Ali flew away.

Rishi wanted to avoid going back to the house. It would take him some time to flush Ali out of his system. He didn't want to sit and mope around the house. So he went for a walk—a long one.

Shehzad preferred going back to his room. Every time he was low or lonely, he locked himself in and let his emotional demons thrash him till they could not hurt him any more. He had ragged the chef the most and would probably miss him the most too. But fuck, everyone left you one day. And who knew that better than him! He shouldn't have let that idiot sneak in so close, within beating distance of his heart—that always caused pain. Lost in thought, he walked up to the door and collided into someone standing there. Damn, who was this now?

'Are you okay?'

Shehzad looked up at the voice and froze. She had not seen his face in the dark. But now, close up, she got a great view, and it nearly stopped her heart. He was the spitting image of her.

She reminded him of someone—himself. The resemblance was unmistakable. That same chin, angular features, even the eyes and hair. Shehzad stood paralysed. This was his home, and she was here. There was nowhere for him to run.

'Shehzad . . .' It took her many minutes before she could get herself to say his name.

'Come in,' was all he said as he unlocked the door.

Switching on the lights, he stood next to a wall and waited for her to say her piece. Thank god, Rishi had opted to take a walk. Shehzad was not good at airing his personal shit with anyone.

She stood there toying with how to start. And where? His resemblance to her was startling. The desi tabloid that carried the compass story with his picture and the TV grabs had not prepared her for this almost mirror-like reflection. 'I . . . I saw you on TV.'

He did not react. The Shehzad of old would have screamed at her to go back to her pilot and not show her mug ever again. But prison had aged him. He was past such shows of grief or frustration.

'You must've suffered so much in there . . .' She couldn't get herself to say that dreadful word 'prison'.

He had suffered much more when he was not even six years old. But he didn't tell her that.

'They showed your compass box on TV.' She took a few steps towards him. 'You still have it. Your birthday gift from me . . .'

There was a bloody battle raging inside him. But on the outside, he looked calm and unmoved. Shehzad was becoming quite an act. Zeenat would've found it tough to believe it was him.

His silence killed her more than his words could have. She dropped down on to the floor and wept. All those tears she had dammed up for years plunged down endlessly, telling their story, seeking forgiveness. 'I was young then, Shehzad,' she tried to explain. 'Too young to understand that one wrong . . . just one wrong can undo every right.'

Shehzad's ears pricked up at that. He still looked away from her. He had done wrongs too—many, in fact—but nothing as bad as her. He'd not hurt anyone.

'I don't expect you to understand,' she said.

But he did. He did not want to, yet he did. It was her measure of wrong against his. That was all. It all boiled down to size. She was gathering herself and trying to get up.

He gave her a hand up.

She had not expected this. It took her a moment to take his hand. And then she could not let go of it, even after she had got up. Her son. Her own flesh. She had craved him so much, over the years, especially as she grew older.

He read it in her eyes then—her need to love and be loved. It was so similar to his own. He saw his emptiness too reflected in him. That broke his restraint, and for the first time in sixteen-odd years, he put his head in his mother's lap and wept. Let go of all the muck that had piled up over the years and was suffocating him.

Rishi returned to a lit-up home with voices coming from the kitchen. One was Shehzad's . . . but the other? It wasn't Zeenat. Curiosity drove him to the kitchen and to a scene of two people who looked like twins—separated by age and gender—cooking dinner and exchanging notes, with such tenderness that it warmed his heart. It took away some of the chill from Ali's departure.

Rishi had been dreading coming back to a quiet and empty kitchen. Not wanting to disturb the duo, he slid out of the kitchen as quietly as he had walked in. But Shehzad was too quick and grabbed him. And then he blushed—Rishi would have bet his last breath on the Bangladeshi never blushing—as he dragged Rishi in and introduced him to his mother.

She stayed alone in Harrow Lane, he told Rishi later that night. The pilot had succumbed to cancer not too long after they married. She was a *Londoni* now, something she always wanted to be. But she was alone—and repenting.

Shutting his eyes for the day, Rishi marvelled at what a day it had been. Ali's dream had been fulfilled. He was gone. And Shehzad's ma had come back. Too much action and emotion it was for normal mortals to endure. He needed to sleep it off.

35

It was not just Desi Beats that was calling him again and again, but even Spicy Talk and Asian Eye. The taint that was likely to make kebabs unpalatable to a customer was a windfall for tabloids peddling sensationalism. All these desi papers rushed to cash in on Rishi's temporary infamy. One wanted him to start a column on the racial issues faced by Asians abroad. Another asked for the story of his imprisonment in lurid detail. And then there were numerous requests for interviews, with one wanting to focus on the relationship he supposedly had with the Labour MP who had batted so devoutly for him.

Rishi was not in a state to oblige any paper or human for that matter. Even the role of agony uncle seemed too painful right now. But he knew he would have to eventually do something. Zeenat could not fund his daily bread and upkeep with another fake hook-up. And Shehzad, he did not want to disturb him. After a lifetime, the boy had found his spot of peace—he deserved to bask in it without Rishi's anxieties.

That left him with just one choice—to leave. He knew how to survive in Agra—for months at a stretch—without working or even thinking of working. But here in London, one needed to toil for every breath. But going back was unacceptable to him. His first promise to not fall in love was gone—Zeenat had seen to that. The second was on shaky legs too. Without wanting to, the arrest had catapulted him to some anti-celebrity status. But the third! The third had been to stay. No, he wasn't going back. Ever.

He let out a sigh and was glad he had come to a decision. The last few notes lurking in his wallet would be needed to fund his tummy till he joined that company in Edinburgh. They had called him again. Well, that was it then. He had to visit Mullah one last time to inform him that one more room in the house would be free to rent out from next month.

The front door, strangely, was half open. Rishi debated whether to ring the bell or not when he heard Fiza shriek. That was definitely disconcerting. She was not one to ever raise her volume. So, what had happened?

'Go! Stop her! She might actually do that . . .'

Next, he heard her weep and wail. Fiza was wailing!

Rishi strode in. Something was very wrong here. The drawing room looked like it had hosted a hurricane. Cushions were flung here, there and everywhere. Place mats had slipped to the edge of tables or dropped down. Fiza's aromatic candles were rolling on the carpet. Even the jade laughing Buddha was askew. Rishi was blown apart.

Mullah sat hunched forward on that tall chair. It was the one Rishi knew Mullah found particularly uncomfortable. And Fiza, she hovered around him like a drone, recording his every move and blink in painstaking detail. Gone were the calm and poise that were known to grace their faces and demeanour. Fiza was ranting and Mullah looked aghast.

He saw the Indian and got up with a start. Grabbing his arm like it was the final straw afloat on the Dead Sea, he said, 'You go get her. She'll listen to you!' He was begging Rishi.

Trying to size up the situation, Rishi got more confounded. That the ruckus was about Zeenat was evident. But what was going on? These two were not in any condition to reveal more. Rishi scratched his head. Now what had this melodramatic dame done this time? With her, it was impossible to say anything. And where was she? Not in the house, he could see.

Rishi went looking for her up and down the street, in the café and the park. Then in the street again, pausing to peek into places she may have huddled into. Her fit of anger could drive her anywhere. He did not try calling her because he knew her phone would be switched off. That was the first thing she did whenever she walked out in a huff, which was often.

'No, she's not come back,' Mullah replied, when Rishi called him two hours later to check. His voice was low and lost.

Rishi was scared now. She played with the old man, he knew. But never went out to hurt him. They were too thick. Despite all the baggage, Zeenat could not live without him. Then what had changed? Where was she?

Shehzad! Yes, he should call him. He might know something. But the tattoo artist was equally at sea.

'I'll wind up this client fast and come home. Okay?'

Good! Now, there would be two of them looking for her. They'd find her, hopefully, in no time. Rishi's mind was going haywire. When it came to Zeenat, logic did not work, and he got hyper even without meaning to.

'Zeenie! Where are you?' he cried out in anguish, as he unlocked his front door and walked in. His words echoed back to him in the empty house. Or wait, was it empty? He felt something . . . felt something move. Who was that crouched behind the three-seater? Rishi switched on the lights. Of course, it had to be . . .

'Zeenie . . . Zeenie . . .' He found her shivering and in pieces. It broke him to see her this way. Gathering her up, without a thought, he held her tightly in his arms, rocking her to calmness. 'Shh . . . shh . . .'

They stayed that way for quite some time. The thought of Mullah and Shehzad made Rishi break his hold on her. He had to call them. But she clung on to him, not letting him shift even a wee bit. So he texted Shehzad, somehow, with half a hand. *She's fine. Tell Mullah.*

It was a long while before her breathing evened out and her frame stopped shaking. Zeenat was not acting today and that's what hurt Rishi the most. Something had broken inside her, something she had not expected to. So used to getting her way that when life raised its ugly, real head, it probably unnerved her.

She wasn't meant for all this. Rishi vowed he would do all in his power to turn her world rosy once more. Whispering soothing nothings into her ears and her hair, he tried relaxing her, and to his surprise, lulled her to sleep. Lifting her carefully so as to not disturb her sleep, he carried Mullah's princess to his room and bed. Lovingly, he slid the sheet over her. This was the second time he was tucking her in bed—though the last time it had been her own bed—yet he had no idea whatsoever where he stood with her. Heck, this was not the time for mushy thoughts. Rishi slapped himself back to the present and walked out to make that call to Mullah.

He bumped into Shehzad who had just entered the house and had a dozen questions bouncing on his tongue.

'Shh . . . she's sleeping.'

Shehzad raced to his room to check on her.

'My room, Shehzad,' Rishi called out.

That stopped him from rushing to her—from assuming things would be the same. Life had changed. He had changed. She would have too. He took a deep breath and went back to the hall. 'I'll . . . I'll let her be . . . she needs to . . .'

Rishi silenced him with a wave of his hand. He was on the phone with someone. 'Yes, I'll see to it . . . Yes . . . sure, I understand . . . No, don't worry . . .'

So Rishi had accepted that agony uncle offer after all. Shehzad felt great. He didn't want to lose Rishi after Ali. And for the Indian to be around, he had to have a job. Grinning, he teased his friend, 'So who you counselling now? Sweet sixteen or her mother-in-law?'

'Mullah,' replied Rishi, sounding serious and preoccupied.

'What the fuck? Even the old man needs you now?' Shehzad was surprised.

Rishi kept quiet. He got another call. Shehzad raised his brows. This Indian was becoming a celebrity of sorts, was he?

'Ali! Janaab, *kaise hain*?' Rishi's mood switched and he put the phone on speaker. The three boys had a rollicking five minutes doing a postmortem of Ali's first few days in Lahore.

'Zeenie? How is she?' asked Ali.

Rishi paused before replying. 'She's got a lot to cope with,' he told him. 'I was just talking to Mullah. All three are breaking.'

Shehzad did a double take. Mullah had called for Zeenie! She wasn't okay! And the old man . . . breaking? And Shehzad, he had been cutting jokes about him. God! He hated himself.

'Ali, you pray for her,' Rishi was saying on the phone.

Shehzad walked up to Rishi's room, opened it without a sound and peeped in. She lay asleep. Her face was slightly pinched as she slept. The tension had not left her completely even now. Zeenat, a worrywart? She had always been the opposite. Always. Shehzad scrunched his face in an attempt to understand. Failing, he left her at it.

36

Rishi was back at Mullah's house the next morning. Visiting him twice in two days, that too with Zeenat not being there, was bizarre. But life was getting stranger by the minute for these South Asians in the island country. So normal was no longer the norm.

'You'll have to give it to her, sir. You know that,' Rishi began in a composed tone.

'But how will that help?' argued Mullah. 'I've said this to her a zillion times. And now you're singing the same tune!'

'Sir, life doesn't always go the way we want it to—you know that . . . you've taken many a tide.'

Mullah kept quiet.

'You owe her this one last thing,' Rishi ventured, exercising even greater caution, not wanting to twist Mullah the wrong way.

'Last thing? But that's exactly what I'm scared of,' replied the father in a rush. 'The minute she knows, she'll take off into the blue, unthinking and foolish.'

'He's right,' added Fiza. She had been listening to the two men speak, not barging in till she had felt the need.

'But you can't stop her,' Rishi pointed out with exceeding patience. 'We all have to make our own mistakes and learn from them.'

Mullah looked up at the young lad sitting in front of him and thought, *What a sane head he has on his shoulders. Zeenat, my baby, needs someone like him.* But he stamped out the idea the second it sprouted. No more. He had muddied his hands enough with that Ali. She was too headstrong to seek his opinion on matters of the heart. But then, wasn't this issue too coming from the same place? Just maybe, this fellow was right? He should tell her. Yes, tell her.

'But Rishi, he doesn't even know what she's asking for,' Fiza pitched in again.

'You surely know something, sir?' Rishi looked incredulous when Fiza insisted Mullah actually had no information. 'It's never like that.'

That was leading. But Mullah chose to ignore it.

'What we know won't help her—it's of no use,' contended Mullah's begum.

'Then we should let her find that out for herself, shouldn't we?'

Rishi's stint as agony uncle was coming in handy now. And it was grating on Mullah's nerves. How dare this twenty-something twit sit and mouth wisdom to him like some enlightened sage! Mullah had conquered the world, and this two-bit idiot was telling him about how to manage his hyper daughter! He would throw him out of his house right now. Not just this one, even 104. That would show him his place.

'Sir, she won't leave you and go.' Rishi had just fired his last shot, addressing exactly the point Mullah was hedging around. And that took him completely by surprise. 'What . . . what did you just say?' cried out Mullah.

Fiza was so surprised that she lost her poise. 'She said that? She actually said that to you?'

Rishi nodded. These two were shit scared of losing her. He had been right. That's what was stopping them from revealing to Zeenat details of her biological parentage. She had screamed, cried, stomped her still-recovering foot and created one hell of a scene. But Mullah and his begum had turned to stone. As long as she didn't know who they were, she had no options to choose from. And would have to remain their princess.

But the logical and cautious side to Mullah still saw shades of grey. 'What if Zeenat has a change of heart?'

'Yes, she does that all the time,' Fiza said, knowing what her husband was fearing.

'She might,' agreed Rishi, 'but that's a risk you have to take.'

The elders were not so sure about this idea now. Rishi shrugged and got up.

Alongside his Zeenat-mad heart, Mullah had a sharp and agile mind too. It spoke to him now. *You lose what you keep by force.* He stopped Rishi and said, 'I'll do as you say.'

Fiza was amazed by this volte-face, but she kept quiet, believing in Mullah's intelligence, as always.

A month later . . .

Rishi was at Mullah's door again, but this time with Zeenat. The two were bidding goodbye before flying off to India. That's where her biological family lived. Mullah had given them the sketchy details he had.

I'll miss you, Mullah wanted to say, but could not. She knew he would. The words seemed unnecessary. But tears were not as easy to hold back as words, and some plopped down, much to Mullah's annoyance. Fiza hugged her daughter tight and made her promise that she would take good care of herself. Both did not quiz her about her return. It was a pact the couple had made to themselves last night.

Zeenat was as bouncy as ever. Her leg had healed completely and there was a shine in her eyes as she was going to revisit her past and explore her future too. It ached her to leave Mullah, but it had to be done. So she made the farewell short. Both said nothing to each other. Just a quick hug.

She was already picking up her bags when Rishi stepped up to shake Mullah's hand. 'You think she'll be back?' He couldn't help but ask the young guy. Fiza looked up at her husband. Mullah did not catch her eye. Quizzing the boy was not barred in their pact.

'Of course she will,' confirmed Rishi, melting at the sadness he saw in the old man's eyes and voice.

'You don't know why she's going, do you?' began Rishi.

'To meet them,' replied the old man, looking pale as death and totally confused .

'Yes. But there's more. Zeenie being Zeenie can't stand someone else deciding for her.'

Mullah could not follow where all this was leading to.

'Giving birth to her had been their choice. Now she wants to exercise hers—by rejecting them.'

Fiza's mouth opened to form a big O. Mullah almost lost his balance.

Rishi smiled. 'Yes, that's what she's set out to do. But don't tell her I told you.'

A week later, at the Taj Mahal . . .

'Slightly to the left, Zeenie . . . yeah, that's fine . . .'

Click.

'What a great shot that was! I got it all . . . the Taj . . . and the river . . . and these . . .'

'I'll click a picture of you both together, sahib. Just for Rs 100.'

Rishi ignored him.

'Please, memsahib, try one at the monument of love! It's not good to click pictures single-single.'

Zeenie pulled Rishi over then and signalled the photographer to go ahead. While Rishi smiled stupidly at the camera, Zeenat had eyes only for him.

His last promise too was gone, broken and forgotten.